Time and Tide

MINDY PAIGE

Cover designed by Pretty Indie

Edited by Jenny Sims (Editing4Indies)

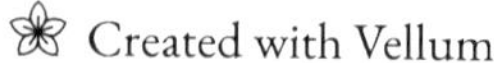

Time and Tide

With her mom passing away and her engagement ending, Amelia Hayes needs a fresh start. A once-in-a-lifetime vacation at a world-renowned hotel in a tropical paradise seems like the perfect way to pull her out of her funk.

There's nothing to derail her plans. Except for the grumpy contractor who loves to torment her.

With his dark eyes and irresistible physique, Ethan Stone is the kind of distraction Amelia doesn't need. Especially since he seems to hate her guts for no good reason.

But Ethan just might be the man to show Amelia all

the things she didn't know she was missing...if he ever stops baiting her.

Chapter One

I STARE OUT THE AIRPLANE WINDOW AS I flick my thumb over the edge of the weathered note in my palm, watching the blanket of clouds slowly roll past my view. The reflection of the early morning light into my half-squinted eyes signals the approach of a brand-new day. Letting out a sigh, I carefully close the shutter and allow my head to loll to the back of my seat, eyes heavy and desperate for rest.

Just as I drift off, a snore explodes from the passenger to my left. My face twists with animosity. I crack my lids and roll my head to the side to give the man a withering glare.

In his unconscious state, he neither notices nor cares about the petite woman sending him death rays. All my pointless glowering seems to do is lull him into a deeper sleep. A puddle of drool begins to run down the side of his mouth, and I sigh, turning back to my window as I resign myself to live in misery for the rest of the flight.

I had paid the extra fee to secure this window seat for my flight to Pebble Beach, which should have been a recipe for success. But due to the sounds exploding from my portly neighbor's mouth, I couldn't sleep, and it was starting to take a toll on my nerves.

I readjust in the seat and feel pins and needles run down my legs, causing me to wrinkle my nose at the irritating sensation.

I could really do with a Xanax right about now.

I groan and shake my head, knowing that I'm being ridiculous. After all, flying has never made me anxious enough to take something before.

I mean, I wouldn't exactly describe what I'm feeling right now as "nerves," but a little something to take the edge off whatever deepened the pit in my chest would be nice. I had gotten used to the fist-sized void that plagued me since Mom passed, but for whatever reason, planning this trip and getting on this plane only served to make it Grand Canyon-sized.

As her memory swirls in my mind, I let out the breath I've been holding in and rest my head back against the seat, allowing my lids to drift closed as I reminisce. She always planned these types of things and was the only one who could make them even slightly enjoyable.

In truth, she had inspired nearly every spontaneous thing I dared to do in my short twenty-four years of life. After all, my mom had been—in every essence of her being—a free spirit. She traveled all over the world before I was born, carrying with her stories and treasures that could have lasted her three lifetimes.

Could have. I repeat to myself as a pang of sadness rings through my chest. I glance out the window, shoving thoughts of her untimely passing away. She had only been gone for six months—coincidently around the same time I ended my engagement—but the pain was still as raw and real as the day she passed.

Instead of moping, I try to conjure up the fond childhood memories I had of us sitting together on the plane; her pointing out the window and exclaiming, "Look out there, Amelia! Wouldn't you love to bounce on those big fluffy clouds?!"

I lose myself to the memory of her kind, shining blue eyes. She had been an exceptional woman; fearless and strong, yet sweet and feminine, with a fiery personality that matched her fiery red curls.

It had been her life's mission to make sure that I lived with the same love for life and adventure that she had, but with my plain brown eyes, cautious disposition, and general distrust of the world, the two of us were opposites, if not for the matching shade of our hair.

Despite our differences, we had been best friends. We didn't really have much of a choice, being that it was just her and me my whole life. My father had passed before I could walk or form real memories, and my mother—a hopeless romantic—resigned to live the rest of her days loving a man long gone.

Her devotion instilled the belief of soulmates into me, and her death gave me the tough realization that I had spent the past three years of my life with a man I didn't truly love. Since I ended things six months ago, I'd thrown myself into work hoping that by staying busy, I'd be absolved of some of the overwhelming guilt racking my gut.

When that didn't work, I'd packed up my dusty bikinis and booked the first flight I could find to Florida.

I'm ripped from my thoughts as a loud *ping* rings over the intercom. I blink up at the flashing yellow seat belt advisory in alarm, completely floored by the fact I had been so lost in thought that I zoned the rest of the flight out.

I have no time to worry about the intense dissociation episode I clearly just experienced because moments later, the sickly sweet voice of the flight attendant rings out over the speakers.

"Ladies and gentlemen, we have been cleared for landing at Sarasota International Airport. Please take your seats and fasten those seat belts as we prepare for landing. Thank you for flying with Star Airlines, and we hope you have a great rest of your journey!"

The final click from the microphone stirs the man next to me mid-snore, and I'm so surprised I choke on my saliva. He blinks lazily ahead, barely even acknowledging my existence as my chest heaves with the effort to clear my lungs.

Well, that checks out. I'm feeling a little bitter as I finally start to get my breathing back under control. He probably kept the whole plane awake with his incessant snoring. Why on earth would he have the decency to care about some chick dying next to him?

With that thought, I shove the note back into my wallet. Then I click my seat belt into place, pulling the strap tight across my waist as I prepare myself for landing; just as the chirpy, body-less voice had instructed.

Sunshine State, don't you dare let me down.

As I trudge through the long hallway toward the pickup spot, I curse under my breath and swing the leather strap of my carry-on higher up on my shoulder. After trying—and failing— to find my luggage for over an hour, an uninterested worker shoved a small slip of paper into my hand and told me the airline would contact me if it ever showed up. With absolutely no hope of that happening, I'm forced to leave the airport with nothing but my carry-on essentials.

You can't call it an adventure without a few hiccups along the way.

The memory of my mom's words and the reason for this spontaneous trip brings me some comfort. My steps lighten as I make my way outside to the oil-stained sidewalk, and I stop next to a leathery-looking couple enjoying a cigarette.

Pulling out my phone, I open a rideshare app, and some of my apprehension dwindles when I note the driver is only five minutes away. The sun-loving duo beside me finishes their cancer sticks and makes their way indoors while I open my messages.

One text from my best friend Elizabeth and several from coworkers wishing me a happy, well-deserved vacation stare back at me as a small frown makes its way onto my face. I hadn't expected to hear from Tom —not after the way we left things—but his absence still brought a little shock to my system whenever I was reminded of it.

Shaking off the thoughts swirling in my head, I text a message to Liz, promising myself to send out the necessary thank-yous to my coworkers when I got to the hotel.

> Hey! Ride is about to get here. Just letting you know I made it off the big metal bird safely. Love you lots!

My rideshare driver pulls up next to me on the sidewalk. The memory of the true crime story "Woman Abducted by Rideshare Impostor" flashes in my mind, and I double-check the license plate on my phone before waving to the driver. Satisfied I'm not about to be axe-murdered, I settle into the passenger seat and take a deep breath, preparing myself for eighteen minutes of small talk.

Well, eighteen minutes was how long it was *supposed* to take to get to the hotel.

Only one road leads to the island, and you have to travel over several rickety drawbridges to make it into town, those of which nearly tripled the GPS time. It wouldn't have been so bad if my driver wasn't so chatty. By the time we stopped at the second bridge, I was ready to sell a kidney to get him to stop talking about his son's Little League stats.

It wouldn't have gotten to me so bad on a typical day. But after a seven-hour flight, limited sleep, and nothing in my stomach except for those stale airplane pretzels, all I wanted was to curl up in some crisp hotel linens and forget the rest of humanity existed.

I let out a deep sigh of relief as the outline of the Grand Flamingo Hotel comes into view. Even in the dusk, the giant pink structure is impossible to miss, and I have to stifle a gasp as the sheer size of it becomes apparent. A spiral stone staircase leads up to what can only be described as a modern-day castle, every inch of which is cast in the most beautiful shade of coral. Huge king palms tower over the courtyard, providing a great deal of shade and giving the whole place the feel of an exotic oasis.

It's hard to believe something so grand and beautiful is hidden in this sleepy little beach town, and even more difficult to wrap my head around the rates they're charging. The website said they were under construction, but you certainly couldn't tell from the outside.

Well, if it looks too good to be true, it probably is.

My ex-fiancé's words ring in my ears as I gaze up at the intricately carved archways, and a pit of dread builds in my stomach. Maybe this is a mistake—maybe I should just tell the driver to head back to the airport and give up while I'm ahead. I don't know the first thing about being alone, and here I am by myself in a strange city, staying in a strange place where the closest person I know is thousands of miles away.

Just then, a horrifying thought comes to mind. *What if the place is haunted or something? A hotel full of angry spirits would certainly account for the price.*

I turn my head to the driver's side, my mouth already in the process of forming the request for him to take me back to the airport. A light tapping on my window makes me nearly jump out of my skin, and I whip my head back to see a joker-like grin on the face of my driver.

My eyes shift from the driver to the suspiciously nice-looking hotel, and I reach for the handle.

Fuck it. I'll take a castle full of ghosties over another hour of small talk any *day.*

THE BEAUTY OF THE OUTSIDE OF THE GRAND Flamingo is really no comparison to the magnificent foyer that greets me as soon as I step inside the lobby doors. Large palms line the walls of the ballroom-esque space, leading up to an ornate reception desk covered completely in iridescent shells. The vaulted ceiling is paneled with sheets of coral-colored glass, casting the room in a soothing warm glow. Several matching macramé hammocks hang from the palms, and a large circular bar stands in the middle of the room, which looks made entirely of crystal. As if that wasn't grand enough, floor-to-ceiling windows make up the back wall of the lobby, showcasing a spellbinding beach-front view.

I walk lightly across the champagne-colored tiles, hearing the click of my shoes reverberate throughout the space as I make my way up to the desk. The place is eerily quiet, and I feel that same tug in my gut, telling me to turn back to my old life of comfort, run out of the lobby, and never look back.

As the thought comes to me, my feet stop short, making a loud squeaking noise against the freshly waxed floors.

"Is someone there?"

A small, weathered voice echoes across the room, and I cringe. Hoisting my bag farther up on my shoulder, I shake off the growing anxiety and force my feet in the direction of the desk once more.

"Hi, yes, I booked a room here?" My voice comes out shakier than I want, and I clear my throat before trying again. "I, uh, booked online. You guys are still open, right?"

A tinkling laugh fills the room. "You must be Ms. Hayes."

I look on in surprise as an elderly woman pops her head up from behind the desk. She was extremely attractive for her age, with tresses of long silver hair secured down her back in a loose braid, piercing baby-blue eyes, and a tanned complexion that screamed "beachgoer."

"Um... yeah." I pause, debating whether I should ask how she knows who I am.

The woman gives me an amused glance. "You're

the only guest I have on the books for today. I wondered when you would finally get here."

The crow's feet at the corner of her eyes deepen as she gives me a kind smile, and for the second time, I'm struck by how blue her eyes are.

"Yeah, sorry about that," I say as I walk the rest of the distance to the desk. "Driving here took way longer than it was supposed to."

Her eyes light up with a knowing look. "Ah, yes. The start of the tourist season really makes traffic a bitch."

I balk at her, unable to help but gape at a woman my grandmother's age dropping a curse like that in casual conversation.

She chuckles. "Sorry, sweetie. Sometimes my upbringing gets the best of me." She shakes her head, causing stray pieces of silver hair to fall around her face. "You'll want to get to your room as quickly as possible after your travels, I'm sure?"

Without waiting for an answer, she snatches a pen and starts writing in a large leather-bound book. I notice the desk is void of a computer, which I'm accustomed to seeing when checking in to a hotel.

My brows scrunch as a horrible thought comes to mind.

"I'm so sorry to interrupt you, but... there *is* Wi-Fi here, right?"

She looks up from her work with a sympathetic look. "I'm sorry, but no. You'll be lucky to get any kind of service out here. Most of us out here still rely on the old landline, if you can believe that."

For the umpteenth time today, my chest becomes heavy at the knowledge of how cut off I really am out here.

I can't help but gulp audibly. "How can that be? How are people supposed to live like that?"

To my surprise, the woman throws her head back with a laugh. "You get used to it. Trust me, dear. I've been working here for quite some time, and I've never had any complaints past the first day."

She gives me another kind smile before ducking from my view. When she reappears, she carefully places a golden key in front of me with the numbers 232 carved into the side.

"Here's your room key. If you need any recommendations on dining, or really great coffee spots, or just getting a feel for the area, I'd be happy to help. Not to toot my own horn, but I really am the person to ask around here. It happens when you stay in a place as long as I have."

Probably realizing I'm about to fall over from fatigue, she finishes her speech with, "Oh, and we serve a free breakfast every morning until ten. It might be my favorite thing about this place besides that view."

She gestures to a hallway leading out of the main lobby. "Now, follow the signs to the West Wing. You have to go up a flight of stairs, and unfortunately, our elevator is currently under maintenance, so the stairs are the only way to get there."

I nod, and she continues. "All but four of our rooms are closed for maintenance at the moment, so you might hear some light construction at certain times of the day. If the noise gets too bad, don't hesitate to call down for a pair of earbuds. My name is Anna, should you need anything else."

So that explains the price drop. I'm not sure if I would rather contend with ghosts now that I know the real reason the place was so cheap.

Taking one more glance around the space, I realize that a little extra noise is a fair price to pay in order to stay in a place as beautiful as this.

I palm the guest key, running my thumb along its teeth as I smile at Anna.

"Thank you," I tell her, secretly hoping I won't need to ask for the sound reducers in question. "I appreciate it."

"Anytime." Anna grins before turning back to whatever she was doing before I came in.

I let out a long sigh as I make my way to the room, thankful I'm only on the second floor so I won't have to drag myself up countless flights of stairs.

Huffing from the effort, I start shuffling down the carpeted hallway, passing countless doors on either side before finally arriving at room 232. As I slide the key into the vintage lock, a drilling sound from farther down the hallway makes me jump, causing the key to fall to the ground. It bounces off the carpet and makes a perfect arc through the air before slipping right under the small crack in the door.

"Shit biscuits," I mutter, crouching to look for the key under the crack.

Shifting my ass in the air, I fold myself onto my forearm and press my cheek against the carpet. The key only made it a few inches past the door, and I think that I might be able to reach it if I can just squeeze my fingers a little bit far—

"Need any help?"

At the sound of the voice, I jump and knock my forehead against the door, hard.

"Fucker!" I screech, reeling back on my heels as I bring a hand up to clutch my head. "Don't sneak up on me like that!"

"I was literally drilling a frame two doors down. It's not my fault your awareness is shit, now is it?"

Feeling white-hot indignation rise in my chest, I whip my head around to face the stranger, fully prepared to rip him a new one for how he's speaking to me.

The man wears nothing but denim jeans, the fluorescent hallway light illuminating a sweat-drenched six-pack and biceps the size of damn watermelons. I let my eyes drag over his perfect frame unabashedly until I reach his face.

My breath catches in my throat as I'm met with brooding, chocolate-brown eyes glaring at me behind a mop of sun-bleached light-brown hair. He looks pissed, and I falter at the look of pure hatred in his eyes.

What the hell did I do to this guy? I think, feeling my brows come together in confusion as he glares at me.

"I *was* going to help you, but I don't really do well with people referring to me as fucker." With a roll of his eyes, he adds, "You're on your own, Freckles."

My mouth pops open in anger. *What the hell is his problem? I wouldn't have called him that if he didn't sneak up on me, for God's sake!*

Just as he's about to disappear around the corner, I call out, "So you're really just gonna storm off? Who the hell shat in your oats this morning, anyway?"

Just as I'd hoped, he stops in his tracks. He turns back to face me, and I have to stop myself from openly staring at his bare chest. He stalks toward me slowly, his eyes darkening with some indiscernible emotion the closer he gets.

Mere inches from my crouched frame, he bends down until our eyes are level with each other. Out of the corner of my eye, I watch a calloused hand swoop toward my face, and I flinch. The stranger's lip quirks up in a tiny smirk, and his knuckles brush my face gently as he guides a few strands of hair behind my ear.

Something roars to life in my chest, and I squeeze my eyes closed to calm my racing heart. A low chuckle sounds near my ear, and his thumb brushes roughly against my bottom lip.

"You think you can get anything you want with that innocent little pout. But I know better." His breath is hot against my neck, and I can't help the small shudder that runs through me. "You're trouble, Freckles. And I'll be damned if I fall for those big brown eyes of yours."

With that, he pulls back with a sneer plastered across his perfect face. "You're a big girl. You can get your own damn key."

Without so much as a glance back in my direction, he straightens up and disappears around the corner for good, leaving me feeling cold, hollow, and a little bit bothered.

"I'll get the key, all right," I grumble, taking the same position and attempting to squeeze my fingers under the door. "Stupid grumpy asshole."

After several failed attempts, I lose hope and fall

back dejectedly on my heels. The top of my hand burns and is turning red from being shoved so roughly against the wood, and the right side of my face has begun to get rug burn. I let out a long sigh and narrow my eyes at the tiny space.

One thing is for sure—I'm not about to let this ruin the rest of my vacation. And I'll be damned if I let that guy get the last laugh.

With a newfound persistence, I position my ass in the air and press my cheek to the floor like earlier, stretching past the point of discomfort until my fingertips finally brush against the cool metal.

"Almost... there," I grunt, using my free hand to force the other farther under the door. Once I have enough leverage over the key, I place my fingers flat over the top and start sliding my hand back out.

"Yes!" I cry, snatching the key from the carpet and holding it over my head in a victory pose. A slow clapping sounds from behind me, and I whip my head to face the same asshole from earlier.

"I gotta say, I'm impressed with your dedication. Most people would just ask for another key instead of putting their pride on the line like that." A muscle in his jaw twitches as his eyes roam over my crouched frame. "Not that I didn't enjoy the view."

What's this dude's issue? First, he's a complete dickwad, and now he's, what? Flirting with me?

My face heats, and I shake the thought away. "Anna told me they were one of a kind, so no, I couldn't just 'get another one.'" The back of my neck heats with anger as another thought comes to mind. "You could have offered to help instead of just watching me like a creep, you know."

The man's jaw ticks again, this time with something more like irritation. "Maybe if you were a little nicer to me, I would have been more inclined," he says, practically spitting out the last word. "And for your information, there is a spare." With a cruel smirk, he pulls out a massive ring of keys from his back pocket. "If you had been a touch nicer, I might have lent it to you."

He rummages through the stack for a few moments before pulling out one identical to mine. He steps forward and hauls me to my feet before I have a chance to disagree, pulling me away from the door and into his chest. My cheek thumps against him, and the scent of sunscreen and cedarwood floods my senses.

"Enjoying yourself, Freckles?" A deep laugh rings out above my head, and I spring backward to put some distance between us. The stranger's eyes shine with amusement as he gestures to the open room door.

My face heats as I look back and forth between the two. *Did I really just* sniff *him? I must be losing my marbles...*

"So... you gonna go inside? You seemed pretty damn determined earlier," he asks, his voice shaking with laughter at my expense.

I narrow my eyes up at him, trying to ignore my racing heart. "I could have done that myself, you know."

He shrugs. "Just trying to be helpful."

I balk at him, feeling a strange mix of fury and desire build in my stomach.

"You know what?" I seethe, brushing past him roughly as I make my way into the room. I stop short once I'm inside and turn on my heels to glare up at him.

"What's that?" he asks, his dark eyes shining with amusement as he stares down at my tiny frame.

"You're a dick," I spit.

Then I slam the door in his stupid, grinning face. Feeling my vision cloud with red, I stomp toward the bed to the sound of his laughter from the other side.

Chapter Three

I'M SO INCREDIBLY ANGRY AS I THROW MYSELF onto the bed, I almost fail to notice the frame has been handcrafted to look like a giant clamshell. The sight makes me smile, dissipating some of my rage from earlier. Fanning my fingers out across the lush white duvet, I nearly moan in ecstasy at how soft the fabric is. I allow my eyes to flutter closed, realizing again how exhausted I am from the journey here.

Just as the wondrous nap is in my grasp, a shrill ringing sound breaks me from my daze, and I bolt upright. I look over in confusion at the hotel phone, alerting me to an incoming call. In an attempt to reach it without actually getting up, I hurl my upper body toward the edge of the bed and reach my arm out desperately toward the bulky device.

"Almost... there..." I grunt, having flashbacks to the

key incident earlier. I cry in victory as I wrap my palm around the phone, followed by a defeated grunt as I topple off the bed and face-plant onto the carpet.

"*Shiiiiit BISCUITS!!*" I roar into the floor, feeling the last of my pride disintegrate into the expensive weave.

"That was so not worth it," I grumble as I bring myself to my hands and knees. "Literally such a bad idea."

The phone still rings, so I reach up and pull it to my ear. "Amelia Hayes speaking. Is there some kind of problem?"

"Dude, I literally thought you were dead." My best friend's sarcastic tone rings through the speakers.

"Liz? Why are you calling me through the hotel landline?" I question, feeling my brows scrunch together as I go to pull my phone out and check for missed calls.

"Oh, I don't know. Maybe because I've been worried sick?!"

Just now remembering the lack of cell service on the island, I whack my hand against my forehead. "I'm so sorry, Liz. I really didn't mean to scare you. I can't get calls or texts out here, and I forgot to let everyone know."

She pauses a beat before asking, "Why the fuck

would you stay in a place without cell service? This isn't the Dark Ages, Ames."

I can't help but roll my eyes. "Honestly, it's been kind of nice not to worry about being glued to my phone twenty-four seven."

"Couldn't be me," Liz deadpans. "Do they at least have like... running water?"

"Oh my God, you're so dramatic." My eyes lift to the ceiling again. "Yes, there's running water, and a huge king mattress, and the most beautiful ocean views I've ever seen. So don't worry about me too much." I chuckle.

"Worrying about you is what I'm good at. Don't you try to take that away from me!"

I pull the phone from my ear with a laugh. "I would never dream of such a thing."

Liz's voice lowers to a hush. "Shit. My manager just walked in. If she catches me on my phone again, I'm so fired."

"Liz!" I whisper-shout, "Why on earth are you calling me from work?"

"I'm sorry, did you miss the part about me thinking you were dead in a gutter? Give me a little slack."

I sigh. "Okay, but please make sure—"

"Okayloveyougottagobye!"

Shaking my head, I place the phone back on the

receiver, then force myself off the bed and start making my way toward the bathroom. I'm wide awake after that call, so the nap will have to wait.

I stare in awe at the giant walk-in shower, not entirely sure what I did in a past life to deserve this on top of everything else. Stripping my shorts and ratty T-shirt in record time, I pull the glass door and hop onto the luxurious tile.

"No way," I gasp, feeling a cozy warmth emanate from the floor. "Heated tiles? What even *is* this place?"

Not wanting to waste another second, I reach my hand toward the crystal knob and turn the water to the hottest setting possible. Nothing is better than a scalding shower, and I had a feeling I would enjoy cooking myself in this one.

I leap back from the showerhead, not wanting to start the experience off with a face full of freezing water. Nothing happens, though, and I stare up at the head in confusion.

"The hell...?" I mutter, turning the knob from left to right to no avail.

I curse under my breath, realizing I would have to call down to the front desk and get this resolved. I hate being a burden, but I'll have to make an exception if it means I get to use the fanciest shower I've ever laid eyes on.

Wrapping a cozy white towel over my chest, I stalk

back to the phone and enter the reception desk number. It barely rings once before Anna picks up.

"Ms. Hayes! Is there something I can help you with?"

"Yes, actually..." I clutch the phone tighter, taking a deep breath to steady my voice before making the request. "I can't seem to get the shower working. Could you... Would you mind sending someone up to look at it?"

"Oh my goodness! I'm so sorry that's happening!" she cries, genuinely upset that I'm dealing with such a small thing, "I'll send someone up right away to take care of it."

"It's okay, really!" I tell her, feeling guilt well up in my chest. "Honestly, you don't need to worry about it. It's probably something I'm doing wrong, anyway."

"Nonsense!" she insists. "We've been having some issues with the pressure in the working rooms. It'll be fixed in no time, Ms. Hayes."

"Thank you so much, really."

"Of course. Is there anything else I can help you with at the moment?" she asks.

"That's all. Thank you again," I tell her, feeling a small smile creep across my face.

"Amazing! Someone will be up shortly, dear." The receiver clicks as she hangs up.

I hug the towel tighter across my body and sigh.

The last thing I want is to hop back into my disgusting airport clothes, but it's not like I have a choice. Cursing my bad luck and the airline under my breath, I start walking back toward the bathroom.

Rap! Rap! Rap!

I nearly jump out of my skin at the loud knocking, causing my towel to fall in a heap in the middle of the floor.

"Shit," I curse. "Just one second plea—"

Without warning, the door to my room swings wide open, and I let out a screech as I attempt to cover myself with my hands. I stare up in mortification at the handsome bastard from earlier, his mouth frozen in a tiny 'o' as he stares down at my naked frame. He seems to whisper something to himself, but I can't quite make it out over the ringing in my ears.

My breath catches in my throat as our eyes meet, and I have to physically remind myself to breathe at the look of pure desire in his dark irises.

"You gonna cover yourself up or just keep standing there like a deer in headlights?"

His cruel taunt snaps me out of my trance, and I snatch up the towel while giving him the mightiest glare I can muster.

"It's not my fault you barged into my room without warning. Who even does that?" I snap.

He crosses his arms over his chest and raises a brow at me. "I did knock."

"Yeah, and I said I needed a minute!" I seethe.

He chuckles at my outburst, and I fight the urge to stomp over and shove my foot between his legs.

"Relax. It's not like it's anything I haven't seen before." He gives me a cruel smirk. "Now, are we done here? I kind of have a shower to fix."

A hollow pang rings through my chest at his look of indifference, but I shake it off and nod.

"Be my guest." I gesture to the bathroom, making sure to keep my voice as icy as possible. *Two can play this game, buddy.* His lips quirk up in a smirk as he brushes past me, and my senses are filled with his scent.

Calm the fuck down, ovaries. I'm slightly irritated that Mr. Grump Grump has this effect on me. I'd been with Tom for three years and never felt anything *close* to what this random stranger did to me.

I let my eyes flit over to where he was working. *Then again, Tom doesn't look anything like that.*

He steps out of the bathroom a moment later, and I quickly avert my eyes to the mattress, hoping he didn't catch me staring.

"Well, you're all set. Nothing more than a simple case of user error." His abdomen strains as he chuckles, and I force my eyes up to his face.

"User error?" I question, squeezing the towel

tighter around my chest as he stands there openly staring.

"Yep," he deadpans. "Come here, I'll show you how to get it running."

"Can't you just tell me?" I whine, not wanting to be stuck in such proximity with him. Certainly not while only wearing a flimsy towel.

He rolls his eyes. "I don't really trust you with spoken instructions. No offense," he adds, looking like he couldn't care less if it actually *did* offend me.

"Whatever," I grumble, standing to trail him into the small space. He steps into the shower and gestures for me to follow.

"I can see from out here," I tell him, crossing my arms protectively over my chest.

"Just fucking get in here," he orders with another roll of his eyes. He grips my arms with his calloused palms, and sparks shoot across my skin where he touches me. Positioning me in front of him, he brushes his bare chest against my shoulder as he places my hand on the shower handle.

Placing his hands on the wall to either side of my head, he leans down until his breath fans against my neck.

"Now," he whispers, "Turn it like you did before. As hot as you want it."

With my heart thrumming wildly, I do as he says.

"Good girl," he murmurs, brushing his lips against my ear. "Now give it a little pull. Gently."

I shimmy the crystal bulb toward me, hearing the water sputter in the pipes the farther I pull. A moment later, cold water streams down on my head, and I let out a loud screech.

"Fucker!" I scream, hopping backward out of the line of fire. To my surprise, the man is no longer behind me, nor does he seem to be anywhere in the bathroom. I look around the space in confusion before letting the sopping wet towel drop to the shower floor.

"Asshole," I grumble, feeling that same hollowness from earlier spread throughout my chest. There's no doubt in my mind that he did that shit on purpose, and I'll be damned if I let him get away with it.

I step under the stream of the now lukewarm water, fuming at the thought of the man laughing at my expense. This was *my* vacation, dammit! I deserve to have a good time without some Thor-looking dickwad messing with my head and ovaries.

I sigh, letting the water pour over my body and wash away all my anger and frustration. It works surprisingly well, and not thirty minutes later, I emerge clean, pruned, and much more relaxed.

That is, until the Post-it note left on my pillow sends me into another fit of rage.

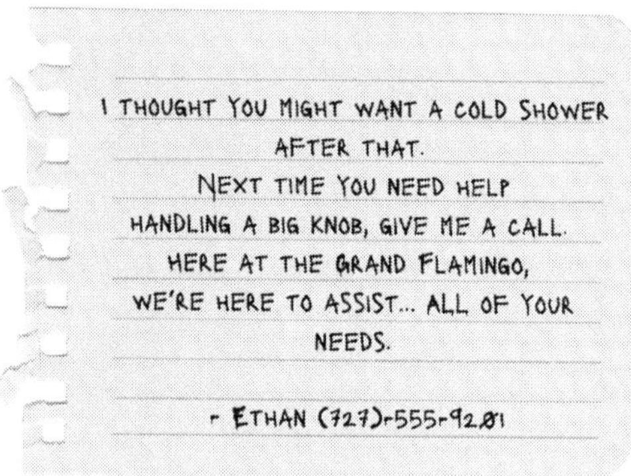
I THOUGHT YOU MIGHT WANT A COLD SHOWER AFTER THAT.
NEXT TIME YOU NEED HELP HANDLING A BIG KNOB, GIVE ME A CALL.
HERE AT THE GRAND FLAMINGO, WE'RE HERE TO ASSIST... ALL OF YOUR NEEDS.

- ETHAN (727)-555-9201

That...that fucking asshole! I seethe, crumpling the note in my palm as I pace the room. *Who the hell does he think he is?*

I look down at the balled Post-it before flinging it against the wall at the opposite end of the room. *Did he really think I would call him after reading his stupid note? Just what kind of woman does he take me for, anyway?*

I continue stomping back and forth across the room, running through all the different insults I'll throw at him the next time we see each other.

If we see each other again, that is. I remind myself, trying not to think too hard about how it makes my heart sink.

With a sigh, I rip off my shorts and shuffle over to the bed, snuggling deep beneath the covers. It's still daylight outside, but the only way to get Ethan off my mind will be through unconsciousness. Closing my eyes, I pull the blanket over my head and feel my muscles relax for the first time since I arrived. I slip into a deep sleep minutes later, my dreams filled with a dangerously handsome man I can't seem to escape.

Chapter Four

A FURIOUS POUNDING NEXT TO MY HEAD startles me awake, and I shoot up in bed with such force that my forehead smacks right into the top of the clamshell.

"Fuck," I hiss, rubbing the tender spot as I blink around the pitch-black space. *What time is it?* My gaze darts over to the electric clock at my bedside, and I'm shocked to see the numbers 3:04 glowing back at me. The rapping starts again, causing me to nearly jump out of my skin as I whip my head wildly from side to side. *What the hell is that?*

With a groan, I throw my arm out to the side to locate the lamp on the bedside table. Still disoriented, I underestimate my reach and send the porcelain lamp toppling to the floor. A loud *crash* sounds out through the space as it shatters into a million tiny pieces, and I cringe to myself in the dark, hoping it wasn't as expensive as it looked. A drilling sound replaces the knocking, and I narrow my eyes as I finally realize what woke me.

Throwing my legs over the side of the bed, I stomp barefoot to my door and throw it open before continuing my march of fury down the hallway to the room next door. Raising my fist, I pound against the wood in quick succession, barely feeling the sting against my knuckles as white-hot rage courses through my veins. I can hear him inside using the drill and pretending not to notice my knocking even as I continue to increase the speed and force. After several more wasted seconds, I reach my limit.

"Ethan!" I scream, the outrage clear in my voice. "I know you can hear me! Open the damn door!" I slam my fist once more against the wood for good measure. "I mean it!"

The drilling stops suddenly, and my heart picks up speed as the sound of footsteps knock heavily against the floorboards, heading toward the door.

The door swings open suddenly, and I stumble backward as Ethan appears in the doorway, droplets of perspiration beading around his bare chest and abdomen. My eyes drift down toward the v peeking out from his low-hanging denim jeans, taking my bottom lip between my teeth as I shamelessly check him out. *God, if only he weren't such a raging dick.*

"What do you want, Freckles?" he barks, glaring down at me with the door clenched tightly in his palm. "I'm right in the middle of something, so make it quick."

"I know that," I snap, the heat in my veins turning frigid at the stark reminder of how much I hated him. "That's why I'm here. You woke me up."

"And that's supposed to be my problem?" he asks, letting out a cold laugh as my face pinches with rage. "Go back to your room and leave me alone." He tries to push the door closed, but I stick my arm through the slot just in time to stop it.

"Ow," I hiss, underestimating Ethan's strength as the edge presses painfully into my flesh.

"Shit! What are you doing?" he curses, throwing the door back open to release me. Before I can blink, he grips my outstretched arm and hauls me into the room. The force of it knocks me off balance, and I stumble forward awkwardly into his chest as he brings my forearm up to his face. His heartbeat thrums wildly against my cheek, and I drag my eyes up, watching him inspect the small red mark with a look of concern across his handsome profile.

"What were you thinking?" he murmurs, lowering his lips to the blemish to place a gentle kiss. With his mouth on me, he freezes, then throws my arm down just as fast as he grabbed it. Shoving me off his chest, he takes a step back, glaring down at me with fire swirling in his dark eyes.

"What the fuck is wrong with you? I could have taken your damn arm off," he growls, shaking his head angrily.

Well, fuck you, big guy. I give him a scowl and cross my arms over my chest, feeling my nipples poking through the thin fabric of the band tee I wore to sleep. My face heats as I glance down at my bare legs, having been so disoriented with anger that I didn't even realize I stood in front of him half naked.

Apparently, Ethan hadn't noticed either. Following my gaze, his jaw ticks as he takes in my toned legs and ass. Letting out a low noise in his throat, he steps toward me, his pupils blown as he rakes his eyes slowly over my body. With a gulp, I retreat from his predatory advance as he herds me into the corner of the room. My eyes go wide as my back thumps softly against the wall, my senses dulling with lust as his face lights up with a smirk.

"Did you really come here just to tell me off, Freckles?" he whispers, reaching a hand up and wrapping it gently around my jaw. He tugs my head up until I have no choice but to look into his impossibly dark eyes, and the starved look that greets me causes me to reel back with a gasp.

"Uh, yeah," I deadpan, forcing my voice to remain icy despite the warmth building between my thighs. "Your stupid hammering woke me up. It's kind of a dick move to be working in the middle of the night, don't you think?" I ask, my tone dripping with malice.

Ethan reels back from me with his usual scowl set in place and a look of pure hatred swimming in his eyes. "You're a real piece of fucking work, don't you think?" he parrots back, looking like he's regretting his previous actions. I don't know why, but the thought makes my heart sink.

"Not as much as you!" I seethe, placing my palms flat against his chest and shoving, hard. Ethan stays put; my efforts just about as effective as a mouse would be against a lion.

"You wanna try that again? Really put your back into it this time." He gives me that infuriating smirk, and I swat at his chest.

"Let me go, Ethan," I order, my breath quickening in my chest as he leans in farther. "I mean it."

"You sure about that, Freckles?" His eyes stay locked on mine as an evil grin works its way across his face. "Because it really doesn't seem like you want me to." Placing one arm above my head to box me in, he trails his hand lightly up the inside of my thigh, stopping at the hem of my shirt to tease the frayed edges between his thumb and forefinger. "I like this a lot," he murmurs, slipping his hand underneath to rest on the crook of my hip. "Such easy access."

My neck heats with a strange mixture of desire, rage, and embarrassment, and on instinct, I try to bring my knee up between his legs. Just before I make contact, he grabs my leg, easily stopping my attack while painfully digging his fingertips into my skin.

"Careful, Freckles," he murmurs, his voice low with a deadly warning. "Don't do something you'll regret."

"Fuck you, asshole," I hiss, trying and failing to wrench my thigh from his grasp. "You're the one who started this."

Ethan chuckles low in his chest, seeming to find my outrage more amusing than anything else. "Still trying to pretend this is all about me waking you up, huh?"

"No one's pretending!" I cry, giving him a look of pure disbelief. "You scared me half to death! I'm going to have to replace that expensive-ass lamp because of *you*!" I seethe, poking my index finger into his chest with a glare.

"So that's what that sound was." Ethan chuckles. "I honestly thought you just got carried away with touching yourself."

"Excuse me?!" I screech. "T-that's preposterous! I don't even do that kind of thing!"

He grins. "There's no need to be shy about it. I bet you look fucking stunning when you come." I choke on whatever I was going to say next, frozen in shock at the words tumbling from his lips. With a devious smirk, he leans in close to my ear, his voice no more than a whisper as he breathes out, "Tell me, Freckles, who is it that runs through that pretty head of yours when you're knuckle deep in your dripping wet cunt? Is it me?"

I gulp as he nips the base of my neck, feeling a shiver run down the length of my spine as desire screams to life in my core. All my other senses dull as he trails his lips across my collarbone, leaving a tiny pocket of fire each place his mouth touches. Just as quickly as he started, he pulls away, leaving me breathless and wanting more despite how angry I had been not even a minute before.

"If you want, I could help you break that headboard of yours, too," he sneers, his icy tone snapping me back to my senses. As I look up into his eyes full of mean-spirited laughter, that same anger from before boils to life in my veins.

"How dare you?" I hiss, shoving my palms back into his chest. "Just who the hell do you think you are?" Taking a single step back, he provides just enough room for me to duck out from under his arm. When we have a few good feet of distance between us, I turn back to face him with my arms crossed over my chest protectively.

"Don't flatter yourself, Freckles," he says, rolling his eyes. "I wouldn't fuck you even if you were on your hands and knees for me and begging for it."

My chest feels hollow as I glare up at him. "Says the man who offered to break my headboard not even two minutes ago."

He shrugs, looking entirely disinterested in the conversation. "Your reactions amuse me. I wanted to see just how much it would take to have you melting in the palm of my hand. Turns out, it's easier than I thought." His laughter comes out cold and hard, and to my surprise, tears well in the corners of my vision.

"Fuck you," I spit, a whirlwind of emotions threatening to break free at any moment. Before they have the chance, I turn on my heel and stomp back out of the room, feeling utterly and completely humiliated by what just occurred. No man has ever made me feel the way he does, completely consumed by raw desire, only to have it dashed a moment later by his cold indifference. *I hate him. I really fucking hate him.*

The thought surprises me, but it rings true in my heart. This vacation was supposed to be an opportunity for me to relax and heal, and so far, it's been ruined at every possible chance. I sigh, dropping my chin to my chest dejectedly as I stand in front of my door. *It's only the first day. There's still a chance for it to get better.*

The thought gives me a sense of hope, and I pull my shoulders back as I turn the brass knob. Locking the door behind me, I carefully make my way over to the bed, making sure to step around the tiny shards of crystal littering the floor. Ripping the band tee over my head, I discard it on the floor with the rest of my garments before flopping backward onto the mattress, my mind racing with unwanted thoughts of the man next door.

At the end of the day, I'm more pissed with myself than him. I don't know why he holds such power over me, but the lack of control I experience every time he's near makes me furious. It's like my brain turns to mush, and all I can think about is how much I want to rip his jeans off and let him take me. My hand trails down my stomach, and I can't help but run my fingertips through the slick arousal coating my inner thighs.

"Shit," I hiss, sliding my middle finger around my clit as his smirk flashes in my mind. I rub my slit gently, my arousal building as I imagine him pinning me down on the bed and having his way with me. A moan pours from my lips as I near my release, my fingers moving furiously in and around my core as my body twitches with desperation.

"Fuck!" I scream, arching back into the mattress as pleasure racks through me. My body twitches in the aftermath as I'm lulled to sleep, the thought of Ethan just on the other side of that wall filling me with a strange sense of comfort. Especially knowing that he probably heard every last second of that, and there wasn't a thing he could do about it.

Chapter Five

SUNLIGHT STREAMS IN THROUGH THE OPEN curtains, illuminating the piles of linens kicked onto the floor during the night. Even with the A/C running full blast, sleeping in the Florida heat for the first time was a struggle—one I don't think I'll get used to during my short stay here. I crack my eyes open unhappily, struggling to come back to the world of the living.

I brush my tangled red mop of hair back off my forehead and open my mouth wide to let out a monstrous yawn. Rolling over lazily, I glance at the alarm clock and gasp at the time displayed by the bright red numbers. If that clock is correct, I'm about to miss breakfast.

Realizing I have exactly three minutes to get downstairs, I spring out of bed in a desperate haze. I stumble around for a few seconds trying to locate my shoes from yesterday, but somehow only come up with one. Thinking quickly, I rush over to my carry-on and rummage through until I find the slippers I brought with me. They're large, puffy, and shaped like turtles, but it's not like I have any other choice if I want to make it down in time.

Feeling slightly ridiculous, I throw on my clothes from yesterday and rush out of the room and down the stairwell toward the lobby. Stumbling down the last step, I look up in dismay to witness a member of the kitchen staff clearing away the last of the breakfast equipment, with not a drop of glorious brown liquid left in sight.

I fall to my knees in the middle of the hallway. "Noooo!" I groan, looking up at the vaulted ceiling as my heart sinks to my feet. "Why? Haven't I been good? Don't I deserve something nice once in a while?"

"My goodness, what's the matter, sweetie?" Anna's concerned voice rings out from across the lobby, startling me out of my misery.

Geez, she probably thinks I'm insane. I cringe to myself as I slowly rise off the ground.

"Sorry... I, uh, overslept and saw that I just missed breakfast." I rub my hand across the back of my neck, embarrassed.

Anna smiles kindly, unconcerned that she just caught me having a tantrum in the middle of the lobby. "Not much of a morning person?" she asks pointedly, no doubt referring to my current state of dress.

"You could say that," I mutter, feeling my face grow hot. "At least without my coffee fix. My mother saw to that addiction."

"Parenting done right, I'd say." She laughs lightly, no doubt trying to distract me from my rising embarrassment. "Unfortunately, once breakfast goes, so does the last of the coffee." She pauses, her eyes apologetic. "But the café right across the street has everything you need, caffeine-wise."

"You're a lifesaver." I grin, feeling my eyes light up at the thought.

"Hey Anna, I fixed that shelf you were talking about in room 212. Was there anything else you..." The gravelly voice I recognize only too well switches from a professional tone to teasing as soon as he notices me. "Now I think I've seen it all. Fuzzy tortoise slippers—what *will* they think of next?"

I grind my molars together and stay perfectly still, refusing to face him and give him the satisfaction of knowing he got to me.

"They're *turtles,* actually. Sea turtles, to be specific, but I wouldn't expect a man such as yourself to know the difference," I quip, giving a little shrug.

Though I can't see his expression, I can almost feel the heat coming off him in waves. "And just what the fuck is *that* supposed to mean?"

"Ethan! Language!" Anna pipes up from behind the desk, looking slightly mortified. "What on earth has gotten into you? I'm so sorry, Ms. Hayes. I—"

"Please, don't worry." I give her a reassuring smile, then turn my head to face Ethan for the first time. "He's just a little pissy that he doesn't know the difference between turtles and tortoises. It's really not that big of a deal."

Looks like I know his weak spot now.

I giggle as I take in Ethan's expression. His jaw ticks as his dark irises shoot flames in my direction, but he doesn't say a word while Anna looks at us.

"I think I'll go get that coffee now. Thank you again, Anna." I smile at Ethan pointedly as I turn toward the exit. Feeling his eyes on me, I do a little jump and click my turtle-clad feet in the air for good measure. Without turning back to see his expression, I step outside and let the door slam shut behind me.

I squint my eyes against the bright midmorning light and curse myself for leaving my sunglasses in the room. I bring my hand up parallel to my brow line, creating some shade and giving my eyes time to adjust to the Florida sun. Peering through squinted eyes, I'm able to locate the crosswalk and make my way across the street to the café.

It's a square, modern building, surrounded by a wraparound patio with a set of newly finished steps leading up to the main entrance. The interior of the building is exposed by crystal-clear, floor-to-ceiling windows wrapping around the entirety of the structure. Out front of the café hangs a large, unadorned white canopy sign, displaying plain black letters spelling out "*The Bean*" in a simple calligraphy style.

After making my way up the steps, I push open the clear glass door and step inside. A large chalkboard hangs behind the counter, decorated with amateur doodles and a daunting list of the roasts, creamer, and syrup options offered. A petite, beautiful black-haired girl looks up to give me a friendly wave before ducking below the counter to retrieve a canister of whipped topping.

"Hi! Welcome to The Bean, I'll be right with you," she calls out, shaking a frosty looking beverage into a large plastic cup. She slides the cup down the granite countertop to a waiting customer before fixing her beanie and flipping her long braid behind her shoulders.

"Hi, what can I get for ya?" she asks, flashing me a bright white smile and looking up expectantly.

"Uh... can I have a sec?" I request more bashfully than I would have liked. "I have the worst decision-making skills."

"Of course!" she chirps. "I'm the same way! Just let me know when you're set."

Just then, the door to the café opens, and a man with cropped blond hair steps inside. Taking my eyes from the board, I turn to face him and gesture for him to step up to the counter.

"You can go ahead." I grin at him. "I might be here for a while."

The man lets out a small chuckle, looking me up and down unabashedly with his light-blue eyes.

"Thank you," he says, stepping forward and pausing beside me. His eyes twinkle with laughter as he looks down at my feet. "I dig the slippers."

My cheeks flush bright pink at the reminder of what was currently on my feet, and I bring my hand up in an attempt to smooth my messy bun.

"Thanks," I quip. "They're all the rage now, you know."

"Oh, and here I thought I was complimenting you on your originality. My mistake," he taunts back, giving me an attractive grin. "In that case, you still make them look good."

With that, he turns to the amused-looking barista and calls out his order. Swiping his card, he makes his way down to the pickup line without even so much as glancing back, leaving me feeling flustered and even more confused as I stare up at the board.

"Still need a little time?" the barista prods with a bemused smile on her face.

"Yeah, sorry," I apologize, feeling my chest tighten as I try to make a quick decision.

"The caramel latte is the best thing here," she whispers, giving me a pointed wink. "It's what your new friend ordered, after all."

"My new...?" I stop short as she gives a pointed look at the blond man waiting on his order. "Oh right...In that case, a latte sounds amazing."

"Absolutely," she replies, reaching for a paper coffee cup and scribbling something with a black pen. "And your name?"

"Amelia." I smile.

"That's such a pretty name!" she exclaims, sliding the cup down to the next station. "I wish mine was pretty. My parents decided on Cassandra," she says, scoffing and pointing at her name tag.

I smile kindly. "Cassandra's a beautiful name, in my opinion."

"Says the chick wearing turtle slippers." She laughs, her thick-winged liner vanishing in the folds of her eyes as she does so. "For what it's worth, I wish I was wearing slippers right now. My feet are killing me."

"Fashionable *and* comfy," I joke back, attempting to smooth my bun back once more.

Cassandra giggles as she taps in my order on the computer. "It'll be right up for you," she says, handing me the receipt and smiling brightly.

"I'm sorry, I don't think I paid you?" I question, my brow furrowing as I palm the receipt.

She blinks at me. "Oh yeah, the guy in front of you paid for yours, so you're all set."

"Oh."

Shoving my five-dollar bill into the large coffee mug next to the register labeled "TIPS!", I slowly walk to the pickup counter and stand beside the man while Cassandra makes our coffees.

Steeling myself, I look over at him.

"Thank you for the coffee. That was really sweet of you."

"Of course." He grins. "I enjoy paying it forward sometimes."

"Oh right, of course," I reply, unable to help the disappointment from creeping into my voice.

"Shawn!" Cassandra calls out as she slides a white paper cup across the counter to him. He reaches out and grabs it before turning back to face me.

"The name's Shawn," he says, shooting me a smile and holding out his free hand. "Though she kind of ruined the introduction for me."

"Amelia," I reply, sliding my hand in his and giving it a shake. "I guess I should also thank you for your order. I kind of got the same thing."

"A great choice," he says, his smile widening. "So... you come around here often?"

I giggle at the lame pickup line, which gives him more confidence.

"I don't normally do this, but you're honestly so beautiful I can't help myself." He lowers his voice to a husk. "Would you...Do you want to go out with me tonight?"

I choke on my saliva.

"I, uh... what?"

"Go out with me. Tonight." He repeats himself, looking haughty at my reaction to his question.

"I, uh..." I pause for a moment while he looks on expectantly. "Sure. Why not?"

"Sweet." His brilliant blues light up at the good news. "Wanna give me your number?"

"I would, but I can't." I shrug as he gives me a confused look. "I'm only here for a week on vacation, so the only way people can contact me is by calling the hotel."

"Ohhhhh." He sighs, looking far more relieved to know I wasn't just dissing him. "Well then, where are you staying?"

I point at the huge pink castle across the street. "Right there, actually."

His eyes widen. "The Grand Flamingo? That place is like, legendary here. Some people wait on a list for *years* to spend a night there."

I shrug. "They're remodeling, so I guess I just got lucky."

"I'll say..." His voice tapers off in amazement. "So how about I just pick you up at your room around eight? That way I can take you out, *and* I get to see their rooms in the flesh."

He gives me a greedy look as his eyes trail over my body, and I have to force my mouth into a smile. *Fat chance of that, buddy. The only way you're getting into my room on a first date is with a sledgehammer.*

Feeling slightly uncomfortable with his newfound forwardness, I snatch my coffee off the counter and hug the cup to my chest.

"How about I just meet you down in the lobby?" I ask, suddenly wishing there was more distance between the two of us.

He shrugs. "Fair enough. Eight o'clock sharp, then." He shines his bright white veneers at me before turning on his heel and stalking toward the exit with a pep in his step.

"Oh, and Amelia?"

"Yeah?"

"Wear something sexy tonight." He smirks, then leaves before I can respond.

A pit forms in my gut, but I shake off the feeling, convincing myself it was merely because I now have to find something to wear for a date.

Oh shit. My eyes widen as the thought takes hold. *What the hell am I supposed to wear?*

Chapter Six

I TREK ACROSS THE STREET, MY STEPS quickening as my predicament becomes more apparent. Throwing open the doors to the lobby, I'm met with Anna's questioning gaze.

"In a hurry, dear?"

I stop dead in my tracks, closing the door gingerly behind me before turning on my heels to give Anna a sheepish grin.

"Sorry. I've had kind of a crazy morning."

"I'll say." Realizing she unintentionally mumbled that part aloud, she quickly fixes her expression back into a polite smile.

"I'm also having a bit of a crisis."

Anna knits her eyebrows together as she takes me in, no doubt trying to figure out *what else* could possibly have gone wrong in the short time I was gone.

"Another one?"

I try to force a laugh, wincing when I realize just how *not* funny I find the situation.

"Okay, hit me with it." Anna shrugs nonchalantly.

Well, you seem awfully calm for someone about to hear about a potential crisis.

I open my mouth to respond, think better of it, and instead go with, "Are you sure you don't mind? I don't want to bother you if you're busy."

Anna chuckles lightly before doing a dramatic scan of the empty lobby.

"You're right. Tons of work to do around here. Why, I wouldn't *dream* of taking a minute out of my busy schedule to listen to a sweet girl's problems. Not for an instant." Her voice drips with sarcasm.

"So what kind of a crisis are we talking about?" she asks, back to her usual politeness.

"Well..." I pause, debating whether it was a good idea to tell her. "I kind of got asked out on a date."

After a few moments of silence, I look up expectantly, only to be met with Anna's puzzled expression.

"I'm still waiting to hear the *crisis* part, hon," she deadpans.

My cheeks flush beet red. "Well, the issue is... I guess the *glaring* issue at the moment is that I don't have a single thing to wear."

At this, Anna breaks into a relieved smile. "Oh,

everyone says that. If you need help picking something out, I'd be more than happy to—"

"No, no, it's not that." I interrupt, holding my palms up apologetically. "I wish it was that, but... I *literally* have nothing to wear. The airline lost my baggage, so all I have is... well, *this*." I gesture down to my ratty jean shorts and tee. "And I don't exactly have the money to replace it."

Anna scrunches her brows in thought, and some of my anxiety fades away. If anyone had a solution to my problem, it was the wizened woman behind the desk.

After a minute, she looks up at me. "Huh. I didn't believe you before, but that really does sound like a crisis."

"I...Wha—" I choke on my spit and send myself into an intense coughing fit. Anna watches me worriedly as I try to compose myself for several seconds.

"Sorry! I shouldn't be so morbid." Anna chuckles tensely. "Don't worry, sweetie. All is not lost."

"It's not?" I sputter, my eyes going wide as I try to take in a breath.

"Of course not!" Anna exclaims, seeming like she's trying to convince us both now.

After another minute of thought, she claps her hands excitedly. "You and I will go shopping together!"

I balk at her, certain she couldn't have forgotten such a large detail so quickly. Before I have time to remind her, she swoops down behind the desk and reappears with a bright red leather handbag. She steps around to my side and pats the top of my hand in a motherly way.

"We'll get you right as rain in no time." She smiles and links her arm with mine. "Now, let's get going. We have to get to the shops and back so you have time to do your hair."

I blink down at the tiny woman as she leads me out of the hotel, wondering if I'm having some sort of fever dream. Even if I am, she's incredibly strong for her age and stature, and I sure as hell don't want to get on the wrong side of her temper.

I sigh under my breath. If she wants to take me shopping, who am I to say no? This vacation is supposed to be about trying new things and growing as a person. One of those things should be learning to accept help from people, right?

Only when we make it outside do I finally find my voice. "You really don't have to do this, you know. It's not that I don't appreciate it—because I really, really do—I just don't know if I feel comfortable having you purchase clothes for me."

Anna gives me a look out of the corner of her eye. "Accepting help from people is a big part of life, Ms.

Hayes. It's better to learn it now than when you're old and gray. Take it from me." She smiles gently as she takes my hand in hers. "If it helps you at all, just remind yourself that you'll be helping *me* by letting me do this."

I open my mouth with a question, but Anna carries on before I have the time to ask.

"I never had a daughter of my own to take shopping." For a moment, emotion wells up in her crystal-blue eyes before she shakes it away. "Plus, I need to get away from this place for a bit. During these renovations, I've been cooped up with hardly anyone to talk to for months."

I pause, knowing I desperately need Anna's help but still not wanting to be a burden to this stranger. Of course, we both know some pretty personal details about each other, so maybe we were more than that now.

"Okay," I concede, giving her hand a slight squeeze of thanks. "Let's go."

"Are you *positive* you don't want to go anywhere a little less fancy? I mean, these prices are—"

"Nonsense." Anna slaps my hand away from the little brown tag displaying a price equivalent to an entire day's salary. "Besides, this isn't any different from the rest of the boutiques on the island."

I stare at her in bewilderment. "How can there be all these places on an island without any cell service? It doesn't seem right."

Anna shrugs as she reaches for a cherry-red minidress. "Politics. They think it'll keep the 'trashy' tourists"—she makes exaggerated air quotes with her fingers—"off the island. And by trashy, all they mean is young. They know how your generation loves their little handheld computers."

I blink at her, unable to fathom the thought process that would lead a team of lawmakers to outlaw cellphones on such a secluded island.

"That's insane," I breathe, forgetting about picking out a dress.

Anna chuckles loudly. "You're telling me. My one pleasure in life was making fun of my relatives' outrageous posts on social media, and now look at me."

She shakes her head. "Wrangling a young woman into shopping with me so I have someone other than Mr. Stone to talk to."

"By Mr. Stone, you mean Ethan?"

She nods before looking off into the distance. "If that man could talk about anything other than drywall and studs, I swear..." Her voice tapers off before she says too much, and I swear I see her cheeks blush the lightest shade of pink.

"Lordy, sometimes I don't know where my head is lately. Here." She thrusts a slinky black bodycon dress into my arms. "Try this one on first."

Not wanting to talk—or more importantly, *think* —about the man in question, I dutifully make my way over to the changing rooms and slip the dress over my head. I'm going on a date with *Shawn*, not Ethan, and I will be damned if I let him control my thoughts for one more night of this vacation.

Without looking at my reflection in the mirror, I shove open the curtain and make my way out to where Anna waits.

"Oh my goodness, you look *stunning!*" Anna cries, nearly dropping the five other garments she managed to pick out in the time it took me to change.

"Thank you," I mumble, feeling my face flush with embarrassment as I spread my fingers over the silky fabric. "Are you sure it's not too much? Too slutty, or—"

"My goodness, you haven't even looked at yourself, have you?" Anna gives me a stern look as she grabs my arm and leads me to the large mirror in the center of the room.

As soon as she spins me around and I see my reflection, I gasp. The dress is perfectly tailored to my frame, hugging each curve and accentuating my frame in ways no other dress ever has. Anna wasn't wrong...I *did* look stunning in it.

"I can't wait to see the look on Ethan's face." Anna grins mischievously over my shoulder. "He won't know what hit him."

"Well, I'm hoping I don't see him at all tonight," I mutter, running my fingers over the fabric and trying to convince myself I mean what I say. "Wait...Did you think I was going out with Ethan tonight?" My eyes go wide in the mirror.

Anna blinks, her face eerily blank as she stares back at me. "I only thought with the way he spoke to you this morning..."

"The guy literally hates me! For no reason, might I add." I balk at her, wondering how on earth she came to that conclusion. *Especially* if she's basing it on our interaction this morning. For chrissakes, the asshole literally made fun of my slippers and swore at me!

"Sorry, dear. My mistake." She pauses, taking in my frame once more before speaking again. "So who's the lucky gentleman?"

I smile at her, grateful we were finally off the subject of the grumpy contractor. "His name's Shawn. We met at the coffee shop this morning."

"And where is he taking you?"

I shrug. "Not sure. Probably a restaurant or something. I'm not expecting anything fancy for a first date."

"Hmm. Of course." Anna drags her eyes over my body one more time. "In that case, you'll want to wear something a bit more modest, don't you think?"

I blink, unable to understand her change in mood. "I thought you loved this one?"

"Well, I did." She smiles, though it doesn't quite reach her eyes. "But it just occurred to me that for a *first* date—like you said—you don't want to give the goods away too soon. Makes you seem desperate."

With my jaw on the floor, Anna returns to the clothing racks, picking from a selection of modest sundresses.

"This one will do." Anna grins warmly as she thrusts a pale-yellow number into my arms. "Try it on for size to make sure it fits you, then we'll get you some regular, everyday items."

I do as she asks without question, not wanting to argue based on her earlier reaction to the black dress. Anna is being gracious enough to pay for me, so I'll wear whatever she thinks is best.

The dress is pretty, although it pales compared to how the other one made me look. Where the other was sultry and revealing, this one is playful and more appropriate for a Sunday brunch than a first date.

Anna likes it, though, so I let her buy it for me along with a few pairs of jean shorts and summery blouses.

Once we make it outside with our arms full of packages, Anna grips my arm, and I turn my head to face her. With tears in her eyes, she gives me a little smile.

"I want you to know how much I appreciate you taking the time out of your vacation to spend an afternoon with me. It means a lot to this old woman."

"Are you serious?" I practically shout, cringing in fear that she might take offense. However, Anna just chuckles to herself and pats my arm fondly.

"I know, I know, I'm the one who bought the stuff. But it was my pleasure, truly." She gives my arm another light squeeze. "You'll understand when you're older. At the end of the day, all we have are the people who remember us. It doesn't matter how much money you have in the bank when we meet our maker. So if I can make the day of a beautiful young woman like yourself, I'll do it. A thousand times over, I'll do it."

I stare at the kind woman, not knowing what to say or how to thank her for what she's done for me. Anna gives me a little wink as if she knows what I'm thinking.

"There's no need to thank me. Like I said, it was *my* pleasure. Now, let's get going. We don't want you to be late getting ready for your date."

Chapter Seven

ANNA AND I STEP THROUGH THE LOBBY DOORS arm in arm, giggling over one of the more memorable stories from her youth.

"So I said to him, 'Bobby, if you really want to kiss me, you'll dive right in that lake and get my scarf back.'"

"He didn't!" I gasp.

"Oh yes, he did." Anna lets out a cackle, her eyes bright with mirth. "He got right in, not giving two hoots about the alligators lounging on the banks."

"So you kissed him, right?"

"Oh, goodness no!" she cries, waving me off as if the question were preposterous. "Although I *did* make out with his brother later that same summer. Now, *that* was a fine man."

"If you thought he was something, you should see

what the younger generation has to offer." I whip my head over to reception and nearly fall over at the sight of Ethan, half naked and lounging lazily against the side of the desk.

"Oh, stop that." Anna giggles, sending a playful wink toward the shirtless hunk. "You're going to give me a heart attack one of these days."

"What? I can't even make an innocent suggestion anymore?" He brings his hand up to his heart, faking a look of hurt as Anna practically swoons in the background.

Jesus, even old ladies have the hots for this guy. I roll my eyes at the thought.

"And just what are you rolling those pretty little eyes at?" Ethan questions, pushing off the desk and stalking over to me. "Come on. Share with the class."

"I'm rolling my eyes at *you.*" I glare, flipping my hair over my shoulder with a huff. "Why don't you get back to your work instead of eavesdropping on our private conversation? That way, you won't have to wake me up in the middle of the night with your stupid hammering."

Ethan's jaw ticks as his dark eyes shoot fire down at me. He opens his mouth to speak but stops when Anna places a weathered hand on his shoulder.

"Ethan, won't you be a dear and take these bags up to Ms. Hayes's room?" she asks, gesturing to the large paper bags in my arms as she expertly changes the subject. His face transforms into a scowl, but he nevertheless takes the bags from my arms.

"What is all this shit?"

"Dresses, shorts, a few pairs of sandals," Anna answers for me, giving Ethan a warning glance. "Miss Amelia has a date tonight, so I thought I would take her shopping for an outfit. Isn't that so *wonderful*, Ethan?"

"Sure," he grunts, frowning down at her with an irritated expression. "Good for her."

Anna bares her teeth at him, the snarl disguised by one of her kind smiles. "Yes. It is, isn't it?"

"So I think I'm gonna head to the pool. I, uh, kinda wanted to try out one of those new bikinis," I mutter, looking back and forth between them uneasily. They're usually so warm with each other, but for whatever reason, Anna seems irate with him after his casual reaction to the news of my date.

"Is that okay with you?" I ask, addressing Anna again when no one answers me.

"Of course!" Anna exclaims, her usually pleasant expression fixed back into place. "You shouldn't even have to ask! Ethan, fish out one of those swimsuits before you take them up, will you?"

Without looking at either of us, Ethan reaches into one of the paper bags and throws a blue string bikini at my chest. I catch the skimpy pieces just before they touch the floor, sending him a glare he pretends not to notice.

"There," he huffs, looking up at Anna. "Now, if you'll excuse me."

"I'll see you later, Ethan." She grins, giving him a little wave of her fingers as he turns and storms off toward the staircase. When he's safely out of earshot, she turns back to me with a knowing grin. "Oh, sweetie, you've got it *bad*."

"Got what?" I grumble, folding my arms over my chest as I stare at the place Ethan stood a moment before.

"Oh, nothing," she replies, her tone flippant. "Forget I said anything...Now, you've still got a few hours before your date. Go out by the pool and relax! I'll have the kitchen send out a drink for you."

"That sounds amazing," I breathe, forgetting about my earlier irritation with the promise of a strong drink by the poolside. "You're amazing. Have I told you that already?"

Anna waves me off with a chuckle, but I swear her cheeks flash with the slightest tinge of pink at my praise. "You're a sweet girl. Now go!"

With a giggle, I do as she says. Strolling out through the sliding back doors, I make my way across the warm stone toward the changing rooms at the far end of the pool. Stripping off my shorts and ratty T-shirt, I pull the light-blue bikini on and step over to the mirror, reveling in the way the silky fabric hugs and supports my curves in the sexiest way possible.

With a newfound confidence, I strut out of the lockers and over to the shallow end, surprised to see a light-pink drink already waiting for me on the side of the pool. Dipping my feet into the cool water, I gladly palm the crystal glass and choke back half its contents. *Much better.*

Breathing in the fresh ocean breeze from the gulf, I slide my lower half into the water and lean back against the tiled edge. My eyes flutter against the sun beating down, warming my pale skin in the cool water. My face works its way into a small smile as I grab my glass, hearing the ice clink softly against the walls as I bring it to my lips. I lay there for a while, sipping my tasty pink beverage and savoring the feeling of calm slowly washing over me, like the tides on the shore less than a mile from where I'm sitting. I close my eyes and listen to them crash against the bank, letting the sounds of the sea lull me into a blissful trance.

A huge crash sounds out across the pool, causing me to nearly piss myself as I flail around the shallow end in a frightened stupor. I swing my gaze over to the source and find myself stunned at the sight of Ethan, shirtless and sweaty with a sledgehammer in his muscular arms. There's a large, hammer-sized hole in the deck where he—no doubt—just slammed the thing, and little specks of rubble line the area around him.

"What the hell are you doing?!" I call, my chest swelling with rage as he ignores me completely, raising the hammer over his head in another mighty down-swing. With my blood pounding in my ears, I jump out of the water and stomp over to him, dripping water across the slick stone tiles the whole way.

"Hey! What in the shit biscuits are you doing?" I ask again, tapping him roughly on the shoulder to get his attention now that I'm close enough.

"What do you mean? I'm working," he growls, still not bothering to look at me. "There was a crack. This whole section has to come up."

My mouth pops open in shock as he slams into the stone again. "Does Anna know you're doing this?"

He shrugs, keeping his back to me as he raises the tool over his head. "She trusts my judgment."

"Well, could you possibly do this—I don't know—literally *any* other time than now?" I ask, trying to keep my voice cool despite the irritation creeping up the back of my spine.

He pauses, turning his head slightly to the side to give me a maddening smirk.

"No."

With that, he carries on, slamming the pavement repeatedly with the hammer until it's reduced to nothing more than a pile of rubble. When he's satisfied with that, he moves on to a section closer to the water, spraying bits of silt and dust all over the poolside and into the chlorinated oasis.

"Are you doing this shit on purpose?" I demand, following him over and standing directly in front of him with my hands placed squarely on my hips. He's fucked with my relaxation, so now I mean business.

"What would possess your pea brain to think that?" he grumbles, raising his eyes to meet mine with a look of pure boredom. "I'm literally just trying to do my job."

"Well, I doubt your job has to do with a microscopic crack in the pavement! No, this—" I pause to make a dramatic circle around his frame with my index finger. "This is calculated. You're trying to get under my skin. I know you are."

"You seem to think awfully highly of yourself," he scoffs, rolling his eyes before turning back to his sledgehammer. "Now if you'll kindly fuck off, I have a lot of work I still need to do here."

His words make me see red. *No one tells me to fuck off. Especially not assholes like him.* Turning on my heel and pretending to storm off, I take a few paces away from him to get a running start. Before he wises up to my plan, I whip back around and charge full speed into his massive side, sending us both crashing into the deep end of the pool.

"The fuck!" he sputters, shoving his sopping brown hair back from his eyes as he surfaces. Seeing me grinning at him just a few feet away, he reaches an arm out, gripping my ankle in his hand before I have a chance to get away. I let out a little yelp as he yanks me toward him, the force of it causing my top to become dislodged and float off behind me. Realizing this, I let out another cry and try to cover myself before Ethan can get a good look.

Wrapping an arm around my back, he hauls my naked chest flat against his with a crooked smile lighting up his handsome features. Reaching his other arm down, he grips my thigh tightly in his palm and bends my leg around his waist. With nothing but the thin spandex of my swimsuit separating me from Ethan's crotch, I can feel practically everything he has going on down there. I gulp, unable to look away from his dark gaze as his cock twitches against my core.

"Is that what you had planned, Freckles?" he questions, his voice husky with desire as he slides his hand back and grips my ass tightly in his palm. "Or were you trying to embarrass me?"

"I-I don't know," I whisper, hearing a whooshing sound in my ears as I stare into his impossibly dark irises. My eyes dart down to his full lips, and my lashes flutter. *I want him to kiss me.* The thought rings out harsh and true in my mind, and I shake my head to clear whatever moment of insanity I must be working through.

Placing my palms against his chest, I shove against him, and thankfully, he lets me go. I kick my feet hard behind me as I paddle in the direction of the steps, too scared to look behind me in case he's hot on my heels. I realize how stupid that thought was as I step out of the water and turn back to see him still in the deep end, lounging on his back without a care in the world.

"What a dick." I curse under my breath, sending one last icy glare in his direction before storming back inside the lobby, one arm crossed firmly over my naked chest. If he won't let me relax, I may as well use all this time to look exceptionally hot for my date. We'll see how the asshole likes me then.

An intense knocking on my door nearly causes me to drop my mascara wand.

"Just a second!" I call, placing the wand back in my makeup bag and walking to the mirror for a final check. After smoothing the pale-yellow fabric back over my knees, I walk over to the door and throw it open.

"Well, hellooooooo, gorgeous." Shawn's bright white veneers nearly blind me with how wide his smile is. "You didn't need to get all dolled up for me."

I give him a quick once-over, noting the flip-flops and graphic tee advertising "Free Dad Jokes."

This *is what he chose to wear on our first date?* I cringe. *I guess I didn't need to go shopping, after all.*

"I thought I was meeting you down in the lobby?" I ask, furrowing my brow in confusion.

Shawn shrugs with that same cheesy grin on his face. "The old lady at reception was nice enough to give me your room number, although..." His voice tapers off. "I guess she had you confused with someone else? No one was in the room she gave me, so I just kinda walked the halls knocking on doors until I found you."

"Huh. Weird," I mumble, stepping out into the hallway beside him and closing the door securely at my back. *Don't want him to get any ideas.*

"Aren't you gonna show me inside?" he asks, unable to hide the disappointed look on his face as the lock clicks.

"Why?" I fire back, blinking up at him innocently.

He stutters for a moment. "Well I...I just thought that since I...You know what? Never mind." He sighs dejectedly. "Let's just get out of here. I'm *dying* for a nice cold beer."

"Sounds good." I force my mouth into a smile I'm not feeling. "Where are we headed?"

"The Crusty Crustacean!" He seems much happier than a moment ago. "They have dollar drafts on Saturday nights."

Great. So we're going to a dive bar. I fight the urge to groan in his face. *Guess that explains the outfit choice.*

"Okay, let's get going," I say as I lead the way down the hallway. *Better to get this night over with as soon as possible so I can enjoy the rest of the night—alone —in bed.*

"Well, well, well. Someone sure cleans up nicely. Nice to see you retired the turtle slippers, Freckles."

My shoulders tense as the familiar voice rings out behind us. I grit my teeth and turn on my heels to face the man who, for some reason, has a hard-on for bothering me.

"Don't you have something better to do besides taunt me?" I snarl, crossing my arms over my chest as he gives me his usual once-over.

Instead of answering, he lowers his gaze to my chest, biting his lip seductively. "I gotta admit, I like the dress. Yellow isn't your color, but you pull it off."

My chest heats as I glare up at him. "You're a dick, you know that?"

"So I've heard." He shrugs. "Though there's not a prettier mouth I like hearing it from."

Before I have the chance to respond, Shawn pipes up, "Um, Amelia? Who is this guy?"

Shit. My eyes go wide as I remember Shawn is still here, watching our interaction.

"He's no one," I mumble, turning away from Ethan to face my date. "Just some guy who likes to piss me off."

"You're a real piece of work, you know that?" Ethan seethes, his fist clenching and unclenching at his side. "Enjoy your date," he spits, then turns on his heel and stomps down the hallway.

I stand frozen where he left me, completely blind with rage as I watch him disappear around the corner. I'm so lost in thought that I almost don't notice the pressure on my arm as Shawn takes hold of me.

"Come on. Let's get out of here, yeah? Don't let that guy spoil your night."

"I wouldn't dream of it," I grumble, shaking my arm loose from his grasp and stomping toward the stairwell. Now, I'm determined to have fun tonight, even if it's with Shawn.

"Wanna 'nother beer?" Shawn's hot breath fans my neck as he shouts into my ear, making sure I can hear his question over the thrumming music. It gives me an icky feeling, and I jerk backward before I think better of it.

He looks hurt by my actions, like a kicked puppy, and the sight makes guilt burn in my stomach.

"I'm good for now!" I yell back, smiling at him to make up for earlier. It works wonders, and before long, Shawn is back to his eager, golden retriever self.

"You sure you don't want another?"

"I'm sure," I say, looking down in disgust at the

lukewarm, piss-yellow beverage sitting untouched in front of me. "Can you get me a shot instead? Tequila, preferably."

If he had a tail between his legs, it would wag a mile a minute. At my request, he grins happily and swoops down to place a peck on my cheek before skipping off to the bar.

As soon as he disappears into the crowd, I let out a deep sigh and lean back against the greasy wooden stool. As attentive as Shawn has been on the date so far, I can't seem to give him the same courtesy. For the whole night, I've felt like I was being watched, but no matter how many times I looked, I couldn't seem to locate the source of my anxiety.

The hair on the back of my neck stands on end, and I whip my head around once more, squinting my eyes in the dim lighting to try to find the culprit. With nothing out of the ordinary, I shake my head, telling myself that it was probably just anxiety from being in a new place.

A minute later, I see Shawn's familiar blond head bobbing through the crowd, and I nearly fall out of my seat with relief. If there *is* an ax-wielding murderer out to get me, at least I can use Shawn as a shield to make a speedy exit.

I look up at his dopey grin as he all but skips toward me. *Hell, he'd probably be happy to take the knife. That, or be a little too dull to figure out what was happening until it was too late.*

"Your beverage, milady." Shawn places a plastic shot cup on the table with a bow. The sight is endearing, and I give him a fake giggle for his efforts.

"Thank you, dear sir." I grin, knocking the bottom of the shot onto the wood before pouring it down my throat in one go.

"*Ahhh.* Cheers." I choke, feeling the liquor burn my chest all the way down. "Is that for me too?" I ask, gesturing to the shot in his other hand.

"Um... Sure." Shawn gives me an awkward smile as he passes it to me. "It seems like you need it more than me."

"Perfect," I breathe, knocking it the same way before taking it down a second time.

"Did, uh... something happen?" he asks, his voice hesitant.

"I'm just peachy," I choke out, sweeping my eyes around the room as my paranoia intensifies. "Actually, do you mind waiting here for a minute? I'm gonna run to the bathroom."

"Yeah, sure," Shawn murmurs, his brows pinched together in confusion as I sweep my legs off the stool and race to the back.

As soon as I'm inside, I race over to the sink.

Placing my palms on the counter, I hang my head to my chest while trying to control my breathing.

"Okay, Ames. Get a grip," I order myself, raising my head so I can stare down my reflection in the mirror.

Geez, I really do look unhinged. I cringe at the frantic mess staring back at me. "No one's out to get you. No one is watching you. You're just *stressed.* You need to take a *chill pill.*"

I sigh, realizing what a freaking nut job I would look like if someone were to walk in right now. Taking my hands off the counter, I straighten up and run them through my messy strands of fiery hair.

After smoothing down some of the frizz, I lean forward and check my eye makeup, nearly jumping out of my skin as the door slams open.

"I'm not waiting! You can go ahead," I call out, placing a hand over my racing heart.

A low chuckle reverberates throughout the tiled walls, and my pulse picks up speed. *It can't be...*

"Thanks for the permission, Freckles."

I whip around, intending to give him a piece of my mind, but I stop short, nearly falling back on my ass at the look on his face. Not uttering a word, he reaches behind him and slides the lock to the bathroom door in place.

"What are you—"

Without warning, he strides up to me, grabs me by the neck, and crashes his mouth onto mine. Warmth floods through my veins at the contact, and I kiss him back without thinking. Much too soon, Ethan pulls back, leaving me flustered and wanting more.

"I wondered what it would take to get you to shut up. Guess I know now." My cheeks flush with embarrassment as he smirks down at me. His look is ice cold, making my chest feel hollow as I stare up at him with unexpected tears blurring my vision.

"I hate you," I whisper, wanting so badly to run away but unable to move an inch under his intense gaze. "What did I even do? Why are you so awful to me?"

"What did you *do*?" His laugh comes out deep and cruel. "Don't kid yourself, Freckles. You know exactly what you did."

"No, I don't!" I sputter, staring up at him with a mixture of fury and disbelief.

Ethan's jaw ticks while he shoves his hands into his hair. "He *had* to take you here. Tonight, of all places," he mutters, seemingly forgetting I could hear every word.

"Who, Shawn?" I question, regretting it as soon as Ethan whips his head back to face me.

"Yes, *Shawn,*" he grits out but refuses to say another word. He starts pacing back and forth, his muscles rippling under his thin white tee and thoroughly distracting me. After a few more moments, he stops, turning toward me and stalking up until we're mere inches apart.

His minty breath fans my face as his chest heaves, and I stare helplessly up at his furious expression, unable to tear my eyes away from his dark gaze.

He brings a hand up to my cheek, running the back of his knuckles lightly along my jawline before wrapping it around the back of my neck. With a tug, I fall forward into his chest and feel the length of his body press up against mine. Still holding me in place, he arches his lips down to my ear, breathing heavily as he places a tender kiss on the curve of my neck.

"I don't like the way you were looking at him." His voice comes out a low husk, and a shiver runs down the length of my spine. "I wanted to kill him. Fuck, I almost did."

His free hand travels up the back of my thigh, stopping short at the hem of my dress to twirl the silky fabric between his fingers.

"I really do like this dress on you, Freckles," he whispers, placing another kiss on the shell of my ear while his hand continues its journey.

"I thought it wasn't my color?" My breath hitches, and I have to bite my lip to suppress a moan as his fingertips brush the edge of my thong. *This guy is seriously confusing.*

With a growl, he digs his fingertips into my inner thigh, causing me to let out a little squeal.

"I'd like it a whole lot better if it was lying in a heap on the fucking floor." He chuckles at my gasp before loosening his grip, letting his fingers continue to toy with me over the thin fabric. "You don't even realize the kind of effect you have. Practically every man in this place has been eye fucking you since the moment you stepped inside with that weasel on your arm."

The pressure around my neck intensifies as he speaks, and I instinctually try to buck against him. He chuckles low in his throat at my feeble attempt and squeezes a little harder, causing a garbled cry to escape as my windpipe closes.

"Where do you think you're going, Freckles?" He pulls my head back so I can look directly up at him, and I gasp at the look of hunger swirling in his dark irises.

Smirking, he slips his middle finger past my thong and dips it into my pussy, swirling gently against my walls and making me cry out in bliss. Sliding a second finger inside, he places his palm flat against my abdomen and curls his fingers back against my G-spot. He starts slowly at first, picking up speed the louder my cries become. Pressure builds in my core the faster he moves, and without warning, my walls collapse around his fingers.

Ethan holds my body upright as my knees buckle, continuing his assault while I explode into his cupped palm and all over the floor. Breathing hard, I clutch Ethan's shirt in my fists and try to regain my footing.

"What...the fuck was that?" I breathe, my eyes opening wide in horror at the mess I made. "There's no way that came from me."

Ethan bellows a laugh, nearly letting his hold on me slip as he throws his head back.

"Trust me, that's all you, baby girl." He smirks before raising his hand up to his mouth, never breaking eye contact with me as he sucks my juices off his palm.

Something in my chest roars to life at the sight, and from the looks of it, Ethan can tell.

"What, you want another?"

"Is that even possible?" My mouth drops as I stare up at him, bewilderment evident across my face.

Before he has the chance to answer, a furious rapping on the door breaks us out of our trance.

"You almost done in there? Some of us need to use the bathroom, too!"

Ethan looks murderous at the interruption, so I quickly place my hand over his chest to calm him down.

"Hey, relax," I mutter, sweeping my arms over his shoulders to hang off his neck. "We can always finish this later..."

Brushing me off, Ethan takes a step back like I just hit him. With an indiscernible look in his eyes, he raises his lip into a snarl.

"Don't count on it," he growls, turning on his heel and storming out of the bathroom without so much as a glance back.

Feeling hollow and utterly confused, I wait a few minutes before following him outside. The asshole from earlier seems to have left, which is good, considering I wouldn't even know what excuse to give them.

I look around the crowded bar for a few minutes, hoping that Ethan stuck around so I can get to the bottom of whatever the hell that was. Shawn has disappeared by this point, too, but it's not like I can blame him. He probably thought I ditched him since I was in the bathroom for so long, and if I'm being honest, a part of me is relieved he did.

With a defeated sigh, I start making my way toward the exit. A good night's sleep is probably just what I need to get over these newfound feelings I seem to have for Ethan.

Although, I have some serious doubts.

Chapter Nine

THE SCENT OF WHISKEY AND SANDALWOOD hits my nostrils, waking me from a dead sleep. My eyes crack open, and I see a shadowed figure hovering above me. His arms are placed on each side of my head, effectively caging me in. Normally, I would be scared, but the man's signature scent fills my stomach with desire instead of fear.

"Ethan?" I groan, my voice groggy from sleep.

Without answering, he leans down to my neck and starts trailing delicate kisses along my bare skin. I let my eyes flutter closed, arching my neck farther to the side to give him more access. He pulls back abruptly, and I let out a little whine before I have time to stop myself.

"Tell me to leave," he grumbles, bringing a hand up and cupping my cheek. "Tell me to go, and I swear you never have to see me again."

What is he talking about? My brain is still fuzzy from sleep, so I shake my head to try to make sense of what he's asking. I look up at him for a few seconds, unable to utter the words.

"Amelia." He lowers his face to mine until our lips are inches apart. "Tell me what you want. I can't leave here unless I know it's what *you* want."

Desire roars to life in my chest, and instantly, I know my answer.

"I want you," I whisper, bringing my hand up and running it across his stubbled jaw. As soon as my skin makes contact, he hisses through his teeth, and his abdomen tightens on top of me.

Without another word, he crashes his mouth onto me, weaving his tongue expertly with mine and leaving me breathless. He nibbles on my bottom lip before taking it between his teeth and pulling it back with a growl.

"Why did it have to be you?" he mutters, reaching up to delicately tuck a strand of hair behind my ear. "Why here? Why now?"

"What are you—" I try to ask but get cut off as Ethan slaps a hand across my mouth. With a murderous gaze, I have a hard time telling who he's more pissed at—me or him.

"Do you even realize what you've done? You've ruined me," he grits out, his jaw ticking with thinly veiled rage. "You and those big brown fuck-me eyes in that tiny little blue bikini."

He rears back, grabbing my hand and forcing it against his bulge with a groan.

"Fuck, even just thinking of it..." His voice tapers off while he continues guiding me, forcing my hand underneath his boxers and wrapping my fingers around his shaft. My eyes bulge as his sheer size becomes apparent, and I let out an audible gulp.

Ethan chuckles low in his throat, his abdomen twitching with pleasure as I continue running my hand up and down his length.

"Jesus, Freckles," he mutters, folding his hand tightly over mine and forcing me to stop the movement. "I don't think I'll be able to stop myself if you keep touching me like that."

"So don't stop," I whisper, feeling a surge of confidence fill my chest as I look up into his blown pupils. "Please, don't stop."

An animalistic growl sounds from deep in Ethan's chest as he reaches down, gripping the sheet from my body and tossing it off into a heap on the floor. My nipples pebble as the cool air hits them, and I let out a little squeal of surprise while instinctually moving my hands to cover my chest.

Ethan's eyes flash with irritation as he rips my arms

away. Gripping both my wrists in a single palm, he holds them above my head, barely even struggling against my resistance.

"I want to look at you." He drags his gaze unashamedly over my bare skin. Still holding me in place, he reaches his free hand up to palm my breast and teases my nipple between his thumb and forefinger.

Dipping his head down to my navel, he lashes his tongue out at my skin before dragging its way up my stomach. I arch my chest up toward him with a whine, desperate to feel his mouth all over me. Chuckling, he pulls away and presses a hand over my chest, forcing me back down to the mattress.

"So goddamn impatient," he murmurs, allowing his hand to trace along the curves of my hip. In the next second, he disappears, and I nearly cry in relief as he reappears at the side of the bed, the belt from his jeans grasped tightly in his palm.

"Come here," he orders, patting the bed for good measure. "I want you to stand here and bend over for me."

My eyes go wide, and he scowls, slapping the belt against his palm.

"*Now.*"

Something about the look in his eyes shakes me to

my core, and I find my body obeying before I tell it to. Placing my feet delicately onto the floorboards, I turn around and lower my chest to the mattress until my skin is flush with the silken sheets. Taking a single step forward, Ethan shoves my legs roughly to the side, making more space for him to position his length between my legs.

The muscles in his abdomen ripple against my back as he leans over the top of me, positioning his mouth at my ear.

"This is going to hurt," he promises, letting out a dark chuckle as my legs shake.

After a moment of silence, a loud *crack* rings through the air. I open my mouth to scream, but he shoves his palm over my mouth to muffle the sound. With his free hand, he reaches back to massage the sensitive area, and I whimper into his fingers, eliciting a wicked chuckle from deep in his throat.

"That was for tonight," he growls into my ear, rearing back for a second time while keeping his hand over my mouth.

"And this"–*crack*–"is for rolling your eyes at me."

The second hit stings more than the first, and tears spring to my eyes as he massages me once more. I've never had a man punish me before, and even though it hurts like hell, I can't imagine myself ever telling him to stop.

"Ethan, please," I beg, my voice breathless from the pain and desire spreading across my skin. "I need to feel you."

"You will," he murmurs, stopping his massage to dig his fingers roughly into my skin. "You still have a few more to go."

I whimper, squeezing my eyes shut tight as the third blow connects with my ass. My skin feels hot but strangely numb, and I'm starting to become addicted to the feeling.

The next two come in quick succession, and instead of screaming from the pain, I find myself holding back a moan as the leather strikes my skin for the fifth time.

"Good girl," Ethan whispers, rubbing my raw skin tenderly with his palm. "Does my good girl deserve a reward?"

I nod wordlessly, my brain far too muddled with lust to form words at the moment. Somewhere in the distance, I hear the clatter of the belt hitting the floor as Ethan bends down, positioning his head between my legs. Tilting his chin up, he teases his tongue inside me before pulling out and swirling it around my slit.

"You taste so fucking good." He darts the tip of his tongue out against my clit. My legs quake as I moan, unashamedly grinding my core backward into his face.

"Please!" I beg, gripping the bed sheet between my fingers. "I need you inside me."

He chuckles, running his fingers down my spine while the other grips his cock, teasing it back and forth through my wetness.

"So. Fucking. Impatient," he growls, placing the tip against my entrance. Unable to wait any longer, he shoves his entire length inside me. The breath leaves my lungs with a gasp. Twisting his fingers in my hair at the base of my skull, he pulls me into a backbend as he yanks my upper body toward him, using my position as leverage to slam in and out of me.

"Fuck!" I scream, feeling my walls constrict around him as he pounds my spot mercilessly. With a few more pumps, stars spark in my eyes as I explode around him, my release soaking his cock and part of the mattress.

"So fucking hot." He pulls out, lowering his head to my pussy to lick me clean. My thighs tremble as his mouth covers the sensitive area, and I try to shy away, but he grips my hips, holding me in place until he's satisfied. Just when I think my legs are going to give way, he resurfaces with his mouth covered in my arousal, highlighting the satisfied smirk on his face.

"So fucking sweet," he murmurs, licking his lips clean.

Hooking his arms under my hips, he tosses me face-first onto the bed before climbing up behind me and shoving my legs apart. I try to flip over to my back, and he smacks my ass in warning, holding me down with his rough palm. Angling his hand, he presses his thumb against the entrance of my ass, and I whimper, not at all used to the strange sensation.

He hums low in his throat as he slowly pushes inside me, sucking a breath in through his teeth as I constrict around him.

"Freckles," he breathes, a hint of reverence in his voice. "You're so fucking tight."

I shove my face into the bed and bite down hard as he starts swirling his digit inside me, stretching me out slowly. He pulls out completely a second later, and I breathe a sigh of relief before the tip of his member presses against me.

"Fuck, I need you," he groans, covering his length with my dripping arousal. Positioning himself once more at my entrance, he pushes the tip inside, and I scream into the mattress, feeling tears run down my face as I'm stretched to the max.

"Shhh." He runs his hand down my spine as he pushes inside me, inch by painful inch. Just when I'm sure he'll split me in half, he stops his assault and starts moving slowly inside me. After a few minutes I start to get used to the feeling of utter fullness, and my jaw goes slack as I let out a loud moan.

Taking this as confirmation, Ethan starts picking up the pace, sliding in and out of me faster and with more force with every stroke. He takes the hand rubbing my back and slides it under my stomach, reaching his fingertips toward my clit.

His fingers on my cunt paired with the overwhelming pleasure his cock brings sends me over the edge, and I arch my back with a scream as my walls clench around him.

"Fuck. Yes!" he groans, moving even faster inside me as he follows with his own release. With a moan, he shoves his hips square against my ass as he comes, his thick cock throbbing against my walls as I seize beneath him.

When he's satisfied, he places a tender kiss on my shoulder blade and pulls out of me. The bed dips beside me as he rolls over next to me, but I'm much too exhausted to move from where he left me.

Luckily, I don't have to. In the next moment, Ethan wraps his arms around my body and hauls me into his chest, placing kisses along my cheeks and forehead as he squeezes me against him.

"You okay, beautiful?" he asks, hooking his thumb under my chin to bring my gaze up to him.

I nod, feeling my eyes flutter with exhaustion. I've

never felt so safe or secure in a man's arms, and right now, all I want to do is sleep.

At my response, he chuckles low in his throat and places another tender kiss atop my head, brushing his fingers through my hair lovingly as I do just that.

Chapter Ten

My eyes flutter against the morning light, and I let out a small noise of discontent before shoving my face into the pillow.

Or at least what my semi-conscious state *thought* was a pillow.

"Good morning, sunshine." Ethan chuckles, reaching one of his massive arms over and pulling me further into his chest. Wriggling against him in an attempt to free myself, I'm met with another chuckle as he tightens his grip, tucking my head beneath his chin.

Goose bumps run across his exposed skin, and he shudders, reaching a hand up to cup my bare breast as his cock twitches.

"Just where the hell do you think you're running off to?" he murmurs, leaning his face to nuzzle my neck. A shudder runs through me, and I try to grab the sheet to cover myself.

"What the fuck are you doing?"

My face heats, and I freeze, dropping the fabric from my fingers instinctually.

"Good girl," he breathes, nipping the skin beneath my ear. Before I can blink, he rolls over top of me, positioning his hands on either side of my head to hold himself up.

His dark eyes search my face the whole time he stares down at me, and I can't for the life of me tell what he's thinking.

"What's up?" I ask, eyeing him with playful suspicion.

"Nothing. Just like looking at you." He grins, reaching up and smoothing my messy red locks back with his fingertips. He dips down to kiss the tip of my nose, retreating out of reach as soon as his lips touch.

"Did... you just kiss my nose?" I ask, my eyes glinting with amusement.

"You bet your ass I did," Ethan deadpans, his eyes alight and daring. "And I'd do it again."

Swooping down once more to peck the tip of my nose, he hooks a finger under my jaw and crashes his lips against mine, flicking his tongue lightly between my lips as he takes the kiss deeper.

A soft moan escapes my throat, and he pulls back with a smug look on his face.

"So... How does coffee sound?" he asks, rolling back off me and swinging his legs over the edge of the bed.

"Not nearly as good as your cock," I grumble.

He chuckles softly, reaching his arms above his head in a stretch. His abdomen and biceps flex as he does so, making him look like something straight out of a sports magazine with the way the light illuminates his physique.

"See something you like?" Ethan's voice breaks me from my trance, and I gulp, pulling the sheet up to cover my bare breasts.

I fidget with the edge of the fabric as he stalks over to her side of the bed, leaning over and taking the side of my face in his palm.

"What the fuck did I say about this?" he growls, lightly raking his nails down my chest until he brushes the edge of the thin white sheet concealing my naked frame.

"Umm," I mumble, trying to remember but getting lost as I stare up at him.

"There's really no point in having a beautiful, naked woman in your bed if you can't enjoy it," he whispers, exposing me fully as he rips the sheet from the bed and tosses it to the floor.

Straightening up, he looks down at my exposed breasts, his eyes darkening with the same ravenous glint I had seen the night before.

"Much better," he growls, his voice hoarse with desire as he leans down once more, covering my mouth with his and kissing me, hard.

He breaks away almost as abruptly as he started, brushing his hair back with his fingertips and grinning down at me, knowingly. He reaches down to retrieve his boxers from the floor and pulls them on, showcasing the biggest tent I have ever seen.

"Be right back, beautiful." He grins at my shocked expression before turning on his heels and leaving the bedroom.

"Oh, and Freckles?"

I jump at the sound of his voice, clearing my throat before shakily calling back.

"Yes?"

"You won't like what happens if that sheet moves from where I left it."

As the door slams shut, memories of last night come flooding in, and cause a small, involuntary shiver to run through my body. I can't remember the last time I've felt this comfortable with someone, much less a complete stranger.

A stranger who you let fuck you. All night.

I shake my head against my intrusive thoughts and

the warmth building between my legs, wishing Ethan would hurry up to continue where we left off last night. Without thinking, my hand slides down between my legs, and I start running my fingers through my wetness, biting my lip to suppress a moan as I tease the sensitive area. I'm so lost in the feeling that I don't even hear the door open or notice the massive man stalking to the bedside.

"Getting started without me, huh?"

I jerk my hand away with a gasp, feeling my eyes go wide as I stare up at Ethan's devious smirk.

"Aw. What if I wanted to watch?"

"Then you should have been quieter," I quip, feeling my cheeks heat as he drags his gaze hungrily over my body spread out on the mattress.

After a minute, he seems to snap out of his trance. Placing the coffee cups down on the nightstand, he pinches his brows with a pained expression.

"I can't do this," he groans, rubbing a hand roughly across his face.

My heart falls at his words, and I instinctively pull my limbs in to try to cover myself. At my motion, his eyes flash with alarm.

"Jesus, not *that,*" he breathes, sitting down on the edge of the mattress and reaching for me. Hooking a finger under my jaw, he draws my head over toward him, his eyes dark and demanding my full attention.

"Then what?"

"Fucking Anna," he whispers, shaking his head in annoyance.

"Anna... the receptionist?" I question, feeling my mouth pull down in a frown.

"Yeah, her," he groans. "When I went down to get the coffee, she asked what we were going to be doing all day. Obviously, I didn't want to tell her the *real* plan," He pauses to give me a pointed look. "So I told her I was taking you out on a date."

Okay, now I'm even more confused.

"How the hell did she know we were... you know, together?" I ask, feeling my face heat with embarrassment at the thought of the sweet old lady knowing what we got up to last night.

As if knowing what I was thinking, Ethan chuckles and softly runs a hand over my arm.

"She has eyes, Freckles. Plus..." He pauses to let out a little laugh. "It's my day off, so there's no reason for me to be here. It's not hard to put two and two together."

"Ah... got it," I mumble, feeling my embarrassment reach new heights. "So what now?"

"Now, I have to take you out, or Anna will physically remove my balls. And I don't think either of us wants that." He chuckles, giving me a dark smirk, "Even though there's nothing more I'd rather do than spend all day in this bed worshiping your pussy."

My body heats with something other than embarrassment, and I have to stop myself from throwing myself at him like a crazed sex addict.

Ethan chuckles at my expression. "Don't worry. I have plans for later tonight, too."

He leans in and places a delicate kiss on my forehead, then reaches over to grab one of the paper coffee cups on the nightstand.

"You'll probably be wanting this now." He grins, placing the cup in my hand and wrapping my fingers around it. "I didn't know how you take it, so I just assumed and added a shit ton of milk and sugar."

"You assumed correct." I smile and take a sip. "Mmm. Delicious. A little coffee with my cream, just the way I like it."

"You know, there's an innuendo to be made there. Someone less gentlemanly than me might even be tempted to speak it."

I raise a brow at him. "A gentleman? You?"

He rolls his eyes at me, swatting my thigh lightly before I have a chance to stop him.

"Watch it," he orders with a growl, but his eyes smile. "I might just have to put you over my knee again if you keep acting up."

My eyes widen, but I say nothing, not wanting him

to realize just how much my body wanted that. My eyes track him as he reaches over and brings his cup to his lips, taking a large swig before placing the cup back with a satisfied sigh.

"Ahh. Bitter and black. Just the way I like it."

I wrinkle my nose. "Gross. My best friend drinks it like that too. She says the more disappointing her coffee is, the more she's prepared for the day."

Ethan barks a laugh, "I think your best friend and I would get along well."

"Can't argue with that. You're both flaming nihilists."

"Watch it," he growls again, though this time it looks like he's holding back a laugh. "We should get ready. I can only control myself for so long, Freckles."

"Where on earth are we going?" I blurt out, unable to keep my curiosity in check for a second longer.

Ethan chuckles, giving my thigh a light squeeze.

"You're pretty impatient. You know that, right?"

"So?" I grumble, crossing my arms over my chest in a mock pout. "You didn't seem to have a problem with it last night."

A single, booming laugh springs from Ethan's

chest. "Someone *really* doesn't like it when they can't get their way."

He reaches over and tries to pat the top of my head, but I swat him away with a glare. Ethan chuckles under his breath before placing his palm back onto my inner thigh, and I have to turn my face away so he can't see my smile.

We drive in comfortable silence for the next few minutes, and I'm struck with how *natural* it feels between us. I can't help but compare it to all the time I spent with my ex, how even a moment of silence felt like it would stretch for days.

My eyes are drawn to the beautiful man at my left, and my chest fills with an unfamiliar warmth as I take in his powerful physique. Feeling my gaze on him, Ethan gives my thigh another light squeeze and sneaks a look at me out of the corner of his eye.

"You okay?"

"Who, me? Just peachy," I respond, shaking my head to clear my wandering thoughts. "Just wondering when we'll get there. You kinda drive like an old woman."

"I have precious cargo to protect." Ethan shrugs with a mischievous grin, and my face flushes. I shake my head, hoping he doesn't realize how much his comment got to me.

"So... are we almost there?" I ask, deciding to change the subject.

Ethan chuckles, gesturing for me to look out the window as he turns on his blinker. To the right is a large glass building with a massive copper sea turtle statue situated in front, the words "Hawthorne Turtle Rescue and Rehabilitation Center" carved into the side of its detailed shell.

I turn to Ethan, my eyes wide with excitement as I bounce out of the seat.

"I thought this might be a fun little date. You know, since you have a thing for the little-shelled bastards." He gives me a pointed look.

I roll my eyes, watching with satisfaction as Ethan's eyes darken at the gesture.

"Now you're just asking to get spanked."

"After we see the turtles!" I cry, giving him my best attempt at puppy dog eyes. "I wanna see the turts."

"Turts?" The corners of his eyes crinkle as he lets out an amused little laugh.

"I said what I said. Now, are we gonna go or not?" I ask, crossing my arms over my chest with a huff.

"You gotta let me park first, Freckles." He chuckles, pulling into a spot and turning off the engine. "So damn impatient."

"Hey, you get what you get, and you don't get

upset." I deadpan, reaching over and pulling the door handle excitedly. "Now let's go, Grandpa!"

He mutters something under his breath I can't quite make out, but with the way his jaw ticks, I can guess it's some punishment he's thinking of dishing out later tonight.

My core warms with the thought of what it might be, and I have to physically shake myself from my thoughts, reminding myself to keep my eyes on the prize.

"Do you think they'll let me pet one if I ask really nicely?"

Ethan shakes his head with a chuckle. "I'm friends with the guy who runs it, so I'm sure we can work something out."

"Ooh, he's sexy *and* has connections," I coo with a wink. "How did I get so lucky?"

Ethan smirks down at me as we reach the door, "You just remember that when your ass is stinging tonight, okay?"

With a light smack, he pulls the door open. "After you, beautiful."

Chapter Eleven

A BLAST OF COOL AIR SMACKS ME IN THE FACE as I step inside, accompanied by a pungent mixture of antiseptic and seawater. We make our way up to the vacant front desk, and I take note of the red, blinking Call Waiting button on the telephone as Ethan peers around.

"Hello? Anyone home?" he calls out, turning back to shoot me an apologetic glance.

"Just a second!" A slightly frantic voice rings out from behind the door marked "employees only."

Moments later, a muscular, dark-haired man comes bursting through the door, wiping his hands furiously on a soiled white cloth. Despite the years swirling in his bright-green eyes, he looks to be a few years younger than me with tanned skin and a lean, surfer's physique.

"Sorry guys, we're a little short-staffed today." He sighs, his biceps straining as he leans his weight against the counter.

Okay, what the fuck are they putting in the water here? I wonder, looking back and forth between the two men. Luckily, the two are too busy exchanging pleasantries to notice me balking.

"All good, man," Ethan replies, a polite smile on his face, "Is your dad around? I was hoping we could see the turtles."

Without a word, the exhausted-looking stranger reaches under the desk and pulls out two wooden clipboards with waivers. "He's out today, so I can take you both back. Just gotta have you sign these, and we'll get going. "

"Sounds good," Ethan responds, taking the boards from his outstretched hand. Then noticing he's made no move toward the phone, Ethan nods his head toward the light. "Aren't you going to get that?".

"Oh, duh!" Jace, according to his name tag, exclaims, immediately jumping forward to pick up the heavy black receiver.

Ethan chuckles under his breath, gesturing for me to follow him over to the couch on the opposite end of the room.

"Hey, sorry I kept you waiting...No, I don't think I

can go out." Jace's low, apologetic voice rings out across the barren lobby.

"I get it, Dad, but I'm literally the only one here today. I wouldn't even be able to get him out of the water by myself and... Yes, really! Well, you're the one who makes the schedule, so I don't see what the surprise is..." He pauses and shoots a look over at us.

"Dude, even if I *could,* I have to give a tour right now. No, I'm not lying. They literally *just* walked in! Well, if you want to try to tell Ethan to come back later, be my guest. What? Yes, *that* Ethan."

Jace clutches the phone tight to his ear, lowering his voice to a flustered whisper as he replies, "No, I can't just *ask him...* Well, *because!!*"

A few moments later, he lowers the phone from his ear, gently placing it back onto the receiver before walking sheepishly toward us.

"Would either of you like to come with me on a turtle rescue?" he asks, the dissatisfaction clear in his voice.

"I'm sorry, what?" I cough out, nearly dropping my clipboard and pen onto the tile below. "We just came in to see the turtles. I don't think either of us is qualified to do that," I respond, my words quickening as I shoot a nervous glance in Ethan's direction.

"It really isn't that hard. We just go out on the boat, pull the little guy up, cut him loose, and we're on our way. Please," he pleads, his eyes wide and hopeful as he addresses Ethan. "It's just me here today, man. You wanted to see the turtles up close, right? What better way than out in the wild?"

Ethan turns to face me, his brows raised in a question. "It's really up to Freckles here."

I look back and forth between Ethan's daring expression and Jace's hopeful eyes, my decision made long ago. With a smirk of my own, I stare defiantly into his dark gaze. "I'm down if you are."

Ethan grins. "You know me, beautiful," he responds, eyes lit up with endearment as he stands, holding a hand out to me for support. "I'm down for anything with you."

"Are you sure this is safe?" My voice can barely be heard over the sound of the motor and the huge crashing waves, so I have to scream my question at Jace. He sits at the wheel with his forearm resting lazily over the top, seeming completely at ease despite the slightly hysterical girl in his ear.

"What?"

"I said, 'are you sure this is safe?'" I try again, closer to his ear.

"Yeah, of course!" he shouts back, patting the edge

of the wheel fondly. "She usually gets us there without any fuss!"

Not the slightest bit reassured, I grip Ethan's forearm even tighter, closing my eyes tightly as we plow through another humongous wave. We had been cruising for quite some time, and by now, the safe oasis of land was nothing more than a speck in the distance. Looking out at the endless void, I can't help but imagine the possibility of a jawed creature popping up to consume the boat and all its tasty passengers.

"Don't worry, I'm sure we're almost there!" Ethan shouts, giving me a quick kiss on the temple. "This is for the turtles, remember?".

Struck with a wave of bravery after being reminded of our mission, I force my eyes open and push away thoughts of being swallowed up by the waves.

"She's right up ahead!" Jace calls excitedly.

Squinting my eyes against the sun, I throw a hand up to shield some of the light and look off in the distance, trying to spot what Jace did. After several moments of searching, a large black object bobbing close to the surface catches my attention.

Jace lowers our speed as we near, letting the boat idle up closer to the mass. I rush to the side of the boat, leaning over as far as I dare to get a better look. A beautiful sea turtle bobs helplessly at the water's surface, ensnared in a sizable black fishing net. My stomach churns at the sight, and my heart aches as I think of how long it must have been out here, struggling to get free.

"Awful, isn't it?" Jace sighs as he reaches over and shuts off the motor. Walking over to stand beside me, he grips the railing and cranes his head over the side to get a better view.

"Yup, it's a bad one." He sighs again. "Welp. Ready to get down there?"

"Why are you asking me?" I ask, feeling my pulse quicken as I look up into his blank stare.

"Um...Why do you think I had you guys put on the wetsuits?" he deadpans.

The light bulb goes off in my head, and I freeze, staring down at my current attire with the most horrible of realizations.

"But...I can't...I mean..." I stutter, looking around the open water in a panic.

"Look, I know it's scary, especially because this is your first time. But I have to man the boat in case we drift too close, and Ethan here"—he gestures to his muscular stature—"has got to hoist the old girl up into the boat."

No doubt noticing my deer-in-headlights look, Ethan walks over and places his hand comfortingly on the small of my back.

"Ames, you know you don't have to do it if you

don't want to... but..." He pauses, looking deep into my eyes with a stoic expression. "That poor thing will be stuck down there and die if you don't. Tell me, Freckles, do you want to disappoint the turts like that?"

Looking between the pathetic, trapped animal and Ethan's infuriating expression, I feel a wave of stubbornness take hold of me.

"Fine. I'll do it," I say, staring stonily up into his dark brown eyes.

"That's my girl." He grins, smacking my ass as I turn back to the edge.

Before I can talk myself out of it, I place my palms on the railing, then swing my long legs over the edge and drop into the dark blue abyss. I surface a moment later, coughing and sputtering, yet overwhelmingly triumphant as I wade slowly toward the mess.

"Don't get too close, you'll get caught in the netting!" Jace calls from the side of the boat. "And keep the splashing to a minimum! Just, you know, not to spook her!"

Taking a deep breath, I feel panic begin to crawl its way up my throat as I reach out, twisting my fingertips in the holes at the edge of the net. As soon as I have a firm grasp, I flip my body around and kick my feet hard to get us back to the boat as fast as possible.

The second my fingertips come in contact with the

smooth hull, I breathe a deep sigh of relief and hold my other hand in the air.

"Nice work, Freckles." Ethan stretches his hand out to me, and I grab hold, letting out a tiny squeal as he effortlessly hauls me out of the water. As soon as my feet touch the deck, my knees buckle under my weight, and I desperately cling to Ethan's forearms.

"I did it," I whisper, half in shock that I just saved the turtle and wasn't devoured while doing so.

"You bet your ass you did," Ethan boasts, squeezing me against his chest and placing a kiss on the top of my head. "Can you stand?"

"Yeah, I think so." I laugh nervously, stepping off to the side so Ethan can haul the turtle out of the water.

With a mighty heave, he manages to get her up against the side of the boat, his biceps straining under the sheer weight of the reptile. After a few more tugs, he manages to slip her over the railing and onto the deck with a massive *thud.*

Wasting no time, Ethan palms the large pocketknife Jace holds out to him and starts hacking away at the thick netting. Wanting to be helpful, I kneel beside them and try to untangle some of the knots constricting her fins.

"Once you get her out, I'll run over and check her. You guys are doing awesome!"

"Couldn't have done it without this one here," Ethan calls to Jace, stopping his work to shoot me a wink.

I return the favor, unable to help the huge grin from forming on my face despite the sad situation before us. As soon as we step back from the net-free turtle, Jace hops up from his seat and switches places with Ethan to examine her, true to his word.

"She looks okay to me," Jace declares, looking slightly shocked. "We're lucky we got to her when we did. Something or another usually tries to take a bite out of them if they're stuck for too long."

Crouching down by the kind-eyed reptile, I reach my hand out and run a finger softly over the edge of her massive shell.

"You hear that? You're a lucky one."

"Did you just talk to the turtle?" Ethan asks, his dark eyes alight with amusement.

"Duh," I quip. "I like her a whole lot better than you right now."

"Ouch," he replies, clutching his chest and stumbling back for dramatic effect.

I scoff, shaking my head as I stand. "You know that's not true."

"Oh, I know." Ethan chuckles, looking me up and down hungrily.

"Uh, guys," Jace interrupts. "Not to be a cock-block, but we kinda need to get her back in the water."

Looking like he wants to reach over and throw Jace in the water instead, Ethan breaks eye contact and crouches down, stretching his arms out wide to grab either side of the giant shell.

The turtle enters the sea with a mighty splash, disrupting the calm surface of the water as she bobs in the same spot for several seconds. Just as I start to worry, I see one of her flippers twitch in the water.

"She's moving!" I yell, rushing over to Ethan and wrapping him in a massive hug.

"And there she goes," Ethan murmurs, wrapping his arm around my drenched suit as he points behind me, calling my attention to the large black mass stream-lining away from us.

The three of us stand watching until she disappears far below the surface and even still after that. Once we know she's gone for good, Jace starts the boat back up and turns us back in the direction of the island.

"Pretty cool, right?" Jace's deep voice breaks the silence.

Craning my head back to the open water, I take one last, fond look.

"*The* coolest," I reply, turning back to Ethan and

placing my lips softly on his. "I wouldn't have wanted it any other way."

The three of us make our way to the employee lockers, desperate to get out of the skintight suits and into comfy, dry clothes. I end up being the last member to reconvene at the receptionist's desk, considering my shower had to be much more thorough than the men's.

"Guys, seriously. I can't tell you how grateful I am. You did awesome." Jace beams at us both.

I shake my head. "Honestly, I think we should be thanking you. That was one of the coolest things I've ever done."

"Same for me, man, and I've done a lot of cool shit," Ethan agrees, grinning as Jace sends him a knowing wink.

"I'll make sure to call you if any other turtles get stuck." Jace sends me a pointed look as he waves goodbye.

We make our way toward the door with Ethan's hand resting protectively on my lower back. He leads me up to the passenger door of his truck, wrapping his hand around the handle like he was going to open the door for me. Instead, he places his hands on either side of my head and presses his chest against my back, effectively pinning me up against the door.

"Don't think I've forgotten about your punishment for earlier," Ethan growls, his voice dangerously controlled as he presses his bulge against my ass.

"Don't think I've forgotten, either," I breathe out, feeling goose bumps rise along my neck wherever his breath brushes.

Feeling, rather than hearing, his chuckle against my back, I nearly fall over as Ethan steps back to pull the door open. Gesturing for me to hop inside, he shoots me a dark grin.

"We better get going, then. Just one more stop along the way."

Chapter Twelve

"THIS WAS A GREAT IDEA," I MOAN, MY MOUTH full of the best cookie dough ice cream I've ever tasted. Like practically everything else on the island, *The Big Scoop* was unnecessarily lavish and extremely enjoyable. It wasn't what I thought Ethan meant when we left the sanctuary, but I was definitely happy when I realized he was taking me for a sweet.

"I'm glad you like it." Ethan reaches forward to wipe off a large dollop that managed to make its way onto my nose. Flushing, I attempt to bat his hand away to no avail.

Taking an enormous bite of ice cream, Ethan leans in and presses his mouth square against mine.

"Look on the bright side." He laughs at my wide-eyed expression before continuing.

"If it's possible, you look even cuter covered in ice cream."

"Oh, you *would* say that." I scoff, rolling my eyes playfully.

"Are you trying to make some kind of *innuendo,* Ms. Hayes?"

Ethan stares me down across the table, his dark eyes alight with the opportunity.

"No, Mr. Stone. I have a strict rule: no innuendos before midnight." I somehow manage to keep a straight face.

Ethan barks a laugh, holding a hand over his chest as he looks deep into my eyes.

"You really are something," he muses, turning his head to look out at the beach. "Your parents are insane, huh? Or at least one is," he states with a boyish grin threatening to take up his whole face.

I cringe, unsure if it's due to the audacity or accuracy.

"I could say the same for you, you know," I quip, not wanting to go into detail and ruin the mood.

Ethan barely pauses a beat. "Nah, mine were definitely more of the deadbeat types."

His tone comes out joking, but I notice that he breaks his usual unrelenting eye contact, appearing to find extreme interest in the tabletop all of a sudden.

"I'm sorry." I speak with raw sincerity as I reach out and place my hand on his.

The action prompts him to look up at me, but instead of seeing the pain from earlier, Ethan is back to his normal self.

"Thank you," he replies, his gaze sincere as he reaches his free arm across, placing his palm over mine to make a sandwich. "You have no idea how much that means to hear you say that."

A soft smile crosses my face as I lean over to place a delicate kiss on each of Ethan's knuckles.

"You still didn't answer the question," Ethan whispers, his voice slightly hoarse. I look up from my handiwork in confusion.

"What question?"

"About your parents. I told you my sob story, so it's only fair."

"Technically, you only told me they were deadbeats. So I really don't think I'm obligated to do anything." I lean back against my seat with a huff.

"I'm sensing some tension."

"No shit, Sherlock."

Ethan's hand twitches on the table, and I let out an audible gulp as I meet his dark eyes with an apology.

"Sorry. I just...I've never really liked talking about it. It makes me uncomfy."

"Uncomfy?" Ethan's previous irritation is gone, replaced with a concerned frown. "Do explain."

I sigh, realizing I might as well bare my soul to the man I was bold enough to bare my pussy to not even twelve hours ago.

"You were right earlier. They *were* wackos. In a good way, I mean." I smile sadly down at the table. "My dad died when I was little, so I don't really remember him too much, just from photos and things like that. And my mom...well, she died a few months ago."

"Oh, Ames, I'm so sorry."

I wave him off, not wanting to let myself feel the emotions welling up from the conversation. "Eh. It's what they're supposed to do, right?"

An unexpected laugh bursts from Ethan's mouth, and I look up in surprise.

"That might have been one of the most morbid things I've heard lately." He shakes his head in disbelief.

I shrug. "What can I say? Dead-parent jokes are always a crowd pleaser."

I let out a laugh, but it sounds hollow even to my own ears. Noticing the change in my mood, Ethan reaches across the table and takes my hand in his. He runs his thumb over my palm, and the feeling pulls me out of my spiral.

As my eyes well up with unshed tears, I turn and look out at the shore to our left.

"You know, it's weird...I keep thinking about how much she would love this place. The sun, the people, the adventure. I can't imagine *she* would ever hesitate to jump in the ocean to rescue a turtle."

"Well, to be fair," Ethan interrupts softly, "you didn't do too much hesitating back there, either."

I pause for a moment, musing, "I guess you're right."

He leans closer with a nod.

"You know, I actually chose this place because I had this memory of her taking me here right after my dad died. It wasn't *nearly* as lavish as now, but I still remember it fondly." I turn, gesturing to the seawall behind us. "One day, we went out on some rinky-dink boat with friends she had made at the bar. They took us to this secluded island that was famous with the locals because it was shaped like a heart, and I spent the day playing with crabs along the rocks while the adults all got wasted. It's stupid, but I remember it being one of the best days of my life." I look out at the water, lost to a faraway memory. "It was one of the last times I remember her being truly happy."

"Are you talking about Lovers Cove?" Ethan interjects excitedly.

"Maybe," I reply, knitting my brows together. "I

don't remember the name of the place. Just that there was this giant cliff face at the center where you could jump off into the inlet."

"Sounds just like it. I'm impressed, my little adventurer."

"Oh no," I deny, shaking my head vehemently, "I never actually jumped off. I was too much of a chicken... probably still am."

Ethan chuckles. "Nah, you just need me there to hold your hand through it," he quips, shooting me a wink and one of his irresistible grins.

Just then, a familiar beanie-clad girl comes bouncing up to the table. Before either of us can say anything, she plops down noisily in one of the empty chairs while shooting us a brilliant smile.

"Hey, stranger." She beams a smile at Ethan as she combs her jet-black bangs away from her eyes.

"Cass," he grumbles, his voice dripping with sarcasm. "So good to see you."

Jealousy roils in the pit of my stomach, and it takes everything I have not to shoot the girl a scathing glare and tell her to buzz off.

"You work over at Beans, right? I'm pretty sure you took my order the other morning."

Cass glances over, sweeping my face until recognition lights up her emerald eyes.

"Slipper girl!" she exclaims, her full attention

focused on me now. "Yeah, I remember you. Oh geez, I'm so rude. I'm Cass, Ethan's sister."

"Sister?" I look between the pair in shock. "I didn't know Ethan had any siblings."

She holds her hand over her heart and gasps at Ethan. "How dare you try to keep me a secret!"

Rubbing a hand across his face, he shoots her a scowl. "Aren't you supposed to be studying for your entrance exam right now?"

"Don't try to change the subject!"

"I'm not," he scoffs. "I just think you should be studying right now."

"Whatever you say, *Dad.*" Cass rolls her eyes. "I wasn't even talking to you. I was talking to..." She looks over apologetically, obviously blanking on my name.

"Amelia," Ethan offers before I have the chance. "And you're kind of in the middle of Amelia's and my *date.*"

"Ohhhhhh, my bad." Cass leans forward excitedly. "I didn't know you were *dating.*"

"Uh, what does that mean?" I ask.

"Nothing," Ethan interjects, holding his hand up to stop Cass from blabbing. "She just likes to embarrass me."

"He's right," Cass relents, her eyes alight with mischief as she stands from the table. "Or... it could be the fact I've never seen my brother take someone out on a real *date* before."

Astonished, I turn to Ethan for confirmation and notice a light tinge of pink spreading across his cheeks. He quickly composes himself, relaxing back into his seat with his usual confident grin.

"I've certainly never been on a date with anyone as beautiful as you," Ethan drawls, shooting me a lazy wink and watching my reaction from the corner of his eye.

"Aw. You guys are so gross." Cass's sarcastic voice pipes up, making me blush fire truck red.

Ethan merely rolls his eyes, returning his attention to Cass as he reminds her, "You can leave anytime you like."

"You're a bully," Cass whines, pushing her bottom lip out in an exaggerated pout. "You know, I *was* going to ask if you were coming surfing with me tomorrow, but now I'm not sure I want your grumpy ass there..."

"I can't anyway. Anna needs me at the hotel tomorrow."

"*Boooo.*" She pouts, crossing her arms dramatically across her chest. "All you ever do is work."

She seems deep in thought for a moment before jumping forward excitedly, taking my shoulders in her hands and leaning forward until our faces are inches apart.

"Will *you* go surfing with me?" she asks, her eyes gleaming in anticipation. "Pretty, pretty pleaseeee? It will be *so* much fun, I promise!"

For a moment, I consider refusing. I've never been surfing before, and the ocean and its contents terrify me. Plus, it's not like I'm friends with this girl, so in reality, I have every right to decline and spend a quiet day in bed like I had planned.

However, one look at Ethan and his hopeful expression shatters all my arrangements. Pushing my doubts aside, I look Cass square in the eyes and force my mouth into a smile.

"You know what? I'd love to."

Needing no further confirmation, Cass steps back and pumps her fist in the air triumphantly.

"Awesomesauce! I'll see you out by the lifeguard post around noon tomorrow?"

By the time I open my mouth to respond, Cass has waved goodbye and skips off happily down the boardwalk.

"Well then..." My voice trails off, equally stunned and fascinated with the whirlwind of the girl who just blew through. "Your sister seems nice."

"Yeah, she's... something," Ethan replies, rubbing his face tiredly. "I'm sorry she roped you into surfing tomorrow. You seriously don't have to go, you know?"

"I know, but I'm actually kind of excited about it."

If I speak it into existence, I hope it will become true by tomorrow afternoon.

"Well, good," he says, the same glint in his eyes from earlier appearing. "In that case, I better get you home. Someone's getting their sea legs tomorrow."

"Well, Freckles, this is where I leave you."

Ethan traps my face between his palms as he leans down to pepper small kisses across my cheeks and nose. When he finally makes his way to my lips, I let out a small moan, feeling my legs weaken the longer Ethan holds me.

"Fuck, I wish I could stay," he groans against my mouth, giving me one more soft peck before finally pulling away.

"You know you always could. It's not like I'd mind."

"Oh, trust me, I know." Ethan chuckles wickedly. "But I have to be up super early to start work on the unfinished wing, and I get this funny feeling that we wouldn't be doing too much sleeping."

Even in the dimly lit hallway, my bright red blush is still wholly visible as he smirks down at me, the expression on his face screaming that he knew *exactly* how his words make me feel.

"I'll just say good night, then," I whisper, fighting the urge to physically drag him to my bed.

"Good night, beautiful." Ethan places one last delicate kiss on my forehead before turning to make his way down the stairwell.

I watch him go for a moment, an unfamiliar longing building in my chest the longer I stand listening to the faint clap of his receding work boots.

Closing the door softly behind me, I lean my head against the solid wood, sighing as I look around the barren hotel room. A familiar black suitcase on the bed catches my eye, and my pulse quickens with excitement. A small white card lies on the luggage, and I palm it quickly to read.

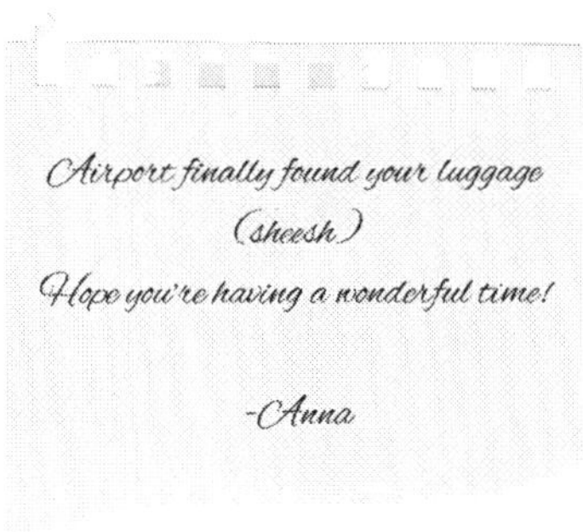

Airport finally found your luggage

(sheesh)

Hope you're having a wonderful time!

-Anna

A smile lights up my face at the note, and I make a mental note to thank Anna in the morning. Tossing the bag onto the floor, I begin getting situated for bed, finally realizing how exhausted I am after today.

A loud knock sounds at the door, and I whip my head over in surprise. With my heart thrumming wildly in my chest, I approach the door. Looking through the peephole, I gasp in surprise and throw it open.

"Ethan," I breathe, my heart fluttering wildly at the sight of him.

"I'm sorry. I don't know what the fuck I was thinking."

Ethan steps across the threshold, taking me in his arms as he crashes his mouth onto mine. With a moan, he slams the door shut behind him and carries me to bed, his heart pounding even harder than mine.

Chapter Thirteen

I SIT WIGGLING MY TOES IN THE SOFT WHITE sand, nervously toying with my wetsuit sleeve as I watch the massive whitecaps crash against the shoreline.

"Don't worry." Cass comes up behind me to place a reassuring hand on my shoulder. "You know all the basics. Now you just gotta get out there and try it for real."

Before I know it, Cass grabs me by the hand and hauls me across the sand toward the ocean, seemingly determined to get me into the water before I talk myself out of it.

Once we're knee-deep, Cass lets go and signals me to follow her lead. I watch in awe as she effortlessly climbs onto her board, lying belly down and using her arms to swim farther out to sea.

"Come on, Ames!" Cass calls, slowing her pace once she notices I still haven't attempted to move.

"I-I'm coming!" My voice is shaky as I crawl onto my board in a similar, far less graceful manner. Once I'm close enough to hear her without shouting, Cass uses her free arm to gesture far out into the distance.

"There's a big one coming. You ready?"

"I sure hope so," I mutter, running over the steps again in my mind.

"Well, whether or not you are, she's coming for you." Cass splashes me playfully before wading away to give me extra space. Not even a minute later, the water crests upward, hurtling a tremendous and terrifying wave straight toward us. I attempt to mirror Cass's actions, swimming fearfully toward the shore as the wave threatens to swallow me whole.

"Look forward!" Cass yells, noticing me watching her movements instead of riding the tide. "You've got this, just let go!"

Following her instruction, I straighten my head and swim with all my might, waiting for the elusive "perfect moment" Cass had told me about. Springing onto my feet, I bend my knees and position myself in the sideways posture Cass made me practice so many times. I look down incredulously, feeling like I'm in a dream.

"I'm doing it!" I call out, astounded. That is, until

the rolling whitecaps clip the front of my board, sending my body somersaulting forward into the water.

I resurface a moment later, coughing up what feels like buckets of salt water as I struggle to find my board. As soon as I get my hands around it, I roll my body over the top and flop facedown while I try to catch my breath.

"You good?"

Cass's voice calls out from the shore, sounding more amused than concerned. Straddling the surfboard, I wipe the saltwater from my eyes and paddle back toward her.

"It's safe to say I've been better!" I call back loudly, making sure Cass can hear every drop of sarcasm in my words.

In response, Cass throws her head back in a laugh, the soft tinkling sound carrying clearly across the distance.

Just like her brother. I chuckle, thinking of the merciless teasing I would have gotten from Ethan if he saw me wipe out just now.

Once I'm safely back on solid ground, I shove the tip of my board into the sand and lean my weight against it while I try to get my pulse under control. As I look over to the left, my eye is caught by a very familiar, shaggy black head of hair.

"Jace?" I call, uncertainly.

The shirtless man stops dead in his tracks, letting the tip of his board pierce the sand as he whips his head around, trying to find the source of the voice calling his name.

"Uh...Hey there?"

Sounding equally as uncertain, he raises his hand up slowly and waggles his fingers in my direction.

Realizing the poor guy probably has no clue who I am, my face flushes with embarrassment.

"It's Amelia from the other day. Remember? The two people you took out to help rescue that turtle?"

"Oh my God!" Jace calls excitedly, recognition finally dawning as he makes his way over to me. "You were that chick I sent into the water with the wetsuit!"

"Yeah, that was me!" I chirp, feeling a smile light up my face. "I jumped in and saved the heck out of that turtle!"

"Yeah, yeah, yeah." Jace returns my cheeky smile. "Man, that shit was *bold*. My dad's been trying to get me to go in the water for *years.* But you have *no idea* how many times I've seen sharks creeping near those turtles, just waiting for an easy snack."

The blood drains from my face, but Jace continues, oblivious and chipper as ever.

"I mean *seriously,* I went home that night and bragged about you guys to my dad. You know what he said? We were probably *juuuust* lucky enough not to—"

"Jace?" I interrupt him, my knuckles white from the death grip I have on the board. "I *really* don't need to know what your dad said."

"Huh. Alright, then." Jace shrugs, reaching up to shove away the messy black hair that had fallen in his eyes.

"Look what the waves dragged in!" Cass calls, sauntering along the shoreline toward us with her board in hand.

Jace's eyes pop as soon as he spots her, and I notice a tinge of red color in his handsome face.

"Cassie!" he bellows, letting his board flop to the sand with a soft *thud* as he spreads his arms wide. Dropping hers in the same manner, she sprints toward him and flings herself through the air before encircling his tall, muscular frame in a koala hug.

"Hi, J," she coos, pulling back and giving him her million-dollar smile. Her dark lashes flutter against the sun as she looks up at him. "Why didn't you tell me you were off today? I would have invited you out with us."

As if realizing I was still here, Cass springs back off him with a gasp. "Oh my gosh, I totally forgot. Amelia, this is my best friend, Jace! Jace, this is—"

“We’ve met.” Jace interrupts, giving me a polite smile.

“We met at the Turtle Hospital the other day,” I explain. Then, noticing the way Cass looks at us, I add, “He even let me get in the water to save one.”

Cass reels back and swats Jace on the shoulder, looking furious.

“Ow! What the hell was that for?”

“You let her in the *water?* Sharks are a real thing out there, you dickwad,” she seethes. "If Ethan ever finds out about this..."

"Ethan was there," Jace deadpans, rolling his eyes at Cass's glare. "You really think he would have let her get in the water if there was any real danger?"

"I guess you're right..." Cass tapers off, shooting him one last withering look before returning her attention to me. "Well, let's get back out there! Ain't no way I’m letting you give up after your first wipeout.”

“Weren’t you *just* talking about the dangers of the ocean? What gives?” Jace whines.

Cass reels around to face him, forcefully shoving her pointer finger into his chest. “There’s a big fucking difference! Why don’t you just go home and think about what you’ve done?”

With a huff, Jace snatches his board off the ground and shoots Cass a glare. Sticking out his tongue, he turns on his heels and starts making his way down the beach, wagging his fingers behind his head in a cheeky goodbye.

"Ugh! He gets on my fucking nerves sometimes," Cass grumbles. "Don't pay any attention to what he said. No one's seen a shark on this side of the island in over a decade, so we're perfectly safe."

Though it doesn't make me feel much better, I decide not to fight her. After what I just saw with Jace, I'm not eager to get on Cass's bad side.

After a few more hours out on the water, we pack it in and slowly make our way back toward the hotel.

"So how are you feeling after your first time out?" Cass asks, wringing out her long black hair on the boards below.

"Honestly"—I sigh—"I can't even believe I did it."

"Believe it." Cass giggles, smacking me playfully on the shoulder. "You were out there shredding waves with the best of 'em. Once I basically forced you out, that is."

"Whatever." I swat her hand away with an eye roll. "Seriously, though...Thank you, Cass. I had a ton of fun."

"My pleasure," she says, grinning ear to ear. "Now you just have to show off your skills on Saturday."

"Saturday?"

"My birthday, silly," she explains, throwing her hands in the air like I should already know this. "Jace is taking us out on his boat to Lovers Cove. It's just gonna be a lowkey day with family, friends, and plenty of booze. You'll be there, right?"

I pause, wondering if anyone on the planet has ever successfully refused this girl.

"Wouldn't miss it."

"Perfect!" She flashes her teeth at me and slips her arm into mine. "You can even make sure Ethan shows up! It's not like he'll miss it if *you're* there."

As she speaks, a thought from earlier enters my mind.

"So I've been meaning to ask you something..."

"About?"

"About Ethan."

From my periphery, I notice Cass raise her brows, intrigued. "What do you want to know?"

"Well, it kind of has to do with what you said last night."

"I've got a big mouth, love. You'll have to be more specific."

I chuckle nervously, feeling Cassandra's prying gaze on me. "What you said about Ethan never dating anyone before... It's definitely giving me some major red flags. I just thought I would ask if there's anything I should be—I don't know—worried about?"

"Oh gosh, you know that was *not* my intention, right?" Cass insists, scrunching her brows in concern. "I just meant that he has trust issues! Big ones...But he's not a sleazeball if that's what you thought I meant!"

I balk at her, not quite sure what to say after all of that.

"Me and my mouth, I swear..." Cass groans, slapping a hand across her forehead. "Look, you really don't need to worry about Ethan. He may be a grumpy asshole 99 percent of the time, but he really is a great man. He raised me, after all, and lord knows that takes a special individual."

I blink down at her slowly. "I didn't know that."

"Really? He's literally *always* in a bad mood. It's like he—"

"No." I interrupt. "That he raised you. I had no idea."

"Huh. I guess that makes sense." Cass sneaks a look at me out of the corner of her eye. "It takes him a while to open up to people. For good reason, at least in his mind. But then, I wasn't old enough to remember most of the shit we went through that made him this way."

“What happened?” I ask. Cass whips her head in my direction, and my face heats with embarrassment.

“Sorry,” I mutter. “You don’t have to tell me anything. It was kind of an insensitive question.”

“Hey, don’t stress. I’m curious that way, too.” She smiles kindly, easing some of my anxiety. “I’m just surprised Ethan hasn’t told you. Though, I guess you guys have been busy doing things other than talking,” she adds with a wink.

My face heats for a completely different reason, and Cass throws her head back in a giggle.

“I get why he likes you so much. You’re a hoot.”

I shake my head. “He definitely likes to push my buttons, that's for sure. Other than that, I’m pretty sure he hates me most of the time.”

“Yeah, I guess you would know.” Cass sighs. “But then again... you haven't seen the way he looks at you when you don’t notice.”

If possible, my cheeks get even redder, and I have to look off to the side to hide my glow.

“Sorry, I didn’t mean to embarrass you.” Cass laughs, nudging my arm playfully. “I just call it like I see it.”

“You didn’t,” I reassure her, continuing the easy pace toward the hotel. After a few minutes of silence, I finally build up enough courage to bring up the past again.

"So... What *did* happen? If you really don't mind me asking, that is."

She smirks at me. "I knew you couldn't resist for much longer. Of course I don't mind. What do you wanna know?"

A loud ding from Cass's wrist tears her attention away from the subject.

"Shit," she curses under her breath, pulling it up to her face to read the time. "I'm so sorry, love. I've gotta run. I'm late for my shift at the café, and my manager will kill me if I track in sand again."

"Don't worry about it," I tell her, though everything in me wants to grab her by the shoulders and shake the story out of her. Instead, I lean in to give her a hug and drop the subject for now. "I'm wiped. I'm probably just gonna head back to my room and crash."

"Jealous," she singsongs before hurrying off in the opposite direction. "Take one for me too, will you?"

"Count on it," I call back, the bed in my room consuming my thoughts as I will my tired legs to make it to the room. As soon as I cross the threshold to the lobby, I take the opportunity to collapse into one of the armchairs by the entryway and breathe a deep sigh of relief.

A booming chuckle sounds from the opposite end of the room, and I shoot upright in the seat, whipping my head around to find the source of the noise.

“Someone looks tired.” Ethan’s voice echoes through the lobby, and I finally spot him climbing down from a ladder in the corner.

“Like you wouldn’t believe,” I reply, unable to help my huge smile at the sight of his muscular frame stalking toward me. Placing his hands on either side of the chair, he leans toward me, kissing my forehead and then my lips.

“I’m surprised to see you back so soon. I thought Cass would have kept you to herself all day,” he murmurs, bringing his hand up and flicking it across my bottom lip as he backs away.

“She had to go to work, so I thought I’d come back here for a nap...” My voice trails off as Ethan descends to my neck, lightly nipping and kissing the delicate skin.

Chuckling, he arches his head up, placing one last kiss along my jawline before standing upright.

“Well, I still gotta finish up a couple of things around here. I’ll be hungry when I finish, so a nap is probably a good idea.” He shoves his hands in his pockets and feigns an innocent expression.

I narrow my eyes. “Somehow, I don’t think we’re talking about food.”

A burst of deep laughter escapes him. “You’re a clever one.”

“Relax, I’m well aware you were making an innuendo," I reply, rolling my eyes against my better judgment.

Ethan hooks a finger under my jaw, forcing my eyes up to meet his. Instead of the anger I expected, his eyes remain soft as he leans forward to kiss me once more.

"You really are something else," he breathes out against me. "I can't wait to see your pretty little face when I throw you over my knee tonight."

I let out a soft whimper as he pulls away, feeling my cheeks turn hot as he gives me a smirk.

"Relax, darling. There's gonna be more of that tonight," he promises, flashing me a wink over his shoulder as he turns back to his work. "Enjoy your nap."

"Count on it," I mumble, doubting I would get a wink of sleep after this. Of course, that was probably his plan all along.

Chapter Fourteen

A SHRILL RINGING SOUND STARTLES ME OUT of my half-awake state, interrupting a particularly explicit daydream I was having about a certain sexy contractor. Letting out a disgruntled groan, I roll onto my stomach and swing my arm in the direction of the phone.

"Hey," I answer, my voice groggy from lack of sleep.

"Ah damn, did I wake you?" Liz's blithe tone rings out against my ear. "I swear, all you ever do now is sleep and fuck. I've never been prouder."

I chuckle, rolling onto my back again and closing my eyes. Apart from a handful of calls to let Liz know I was alive and well, the two of us haven't spoken. At least not to the caliber I'm accustomed to.

"I'm glad I could make you proud," I respond, shaking thoughts of Ethan from my mind. "How have you been? I'm sorry I haven't checked in much. I've just been..."

"Busy. I know." Liz giggles.

From her tone, I know Liz wears that knowing smirk across her face.

"So how is it?" she asks.

"Honestly," I begin, a smile in my voice, "I've never been with a man like him before. It's—"

"Awesome?" Liz interrupts with a chuckle.

Though I know she can't see it, I roll my eyes. "Yeah, you kind of took the words—"

"Right out of your mouth?"

"Would you stop doing that?"

"Stop doing what?"

"*That.*"

"*Whaaat?*"

I pause, bringing my hand up to my brow and applying pressure. I love my best friend to death, but I definitely did not have the energy for her antics right now.

"Did you have anything else you needed? If not, my nap is calling my name right now."

There's a long pause on the opposite end.

"Hello?"

"Oh, hi, I'm still here," Liz responds breathily. The line goes silent once more, save for the muffled sounds of rustling in the distance.

"Uh, Liz?" I ask again, wondering what in the world she got into.

"I'm still here!" Liz calls, seeming like she's farther away from the phone now. "Sorry, I'm just trying to pull these boxes out—"

Her voice is drowned out by a cacophony of crashes, followed by yet another worrying silence. Just as I contemplate calling an ambulance, her chipper voice breaks out through the speaker.

"Hey, sorry about that," she blurts. "Tom dropped off some boxes, and I was pulling them out to see if you wanted any."

At the mention of my ex-fiancé, I expect to feel my stomach drop the way it's described in movies and books. Instead, I'm left with a sensation similar to when you look outside and notice it's going to rain.

"Well, what's in the boxes?" I ask, letting my curiosity get the better of me.

"Looks like photographs, old men's T-shirts, things like that."

I sigh deeply, feeling the bitterness build in my tone as I spit, "Great. So he packed up everything that reminded him of me and left me to deal with it. Real nice guy."

"I'm sorry, hun." Liz's soft, empathetic voice resonates through the speaker. "I shouldn't have brought it up. I wasn't even thinking."

"No, it's good you did," I assure her, "He still tries to find ways to get to me. Even when I'm thousands of miles away, apparently."

"You can't really blame the guy. You're a catch," Liz teases, obviously hoping to brighten the mood.

"Whatever you say," I roll my eyes dramatically, shaking my head to clear the earlier thoughts. Remembering Liz can't see me, I add, "I'm rolling my eyes right now, just so you know."

Liz lets out a seal-like cackle. "Thanks for letting me know."

"Anytime." I glance at the alarm clock beside me to check the time. "Now I really do have to go. Ethan is getting off in a bit and taking me out."

"Ooo, la, la," Liz coos playfully, "I'll leave you to it, then. And don't worry about the boxes, Ames, I'll take care of it."

"Are you sure?"

"One thousand percent. These boxes have a date with the dumpster if you know what I mean."

At this, I laugh wholeheartedly. "You're my favorite. You know that?"

"I better be," Liz quips. "Now go get ready. Have

fun getting off when he gets off, or whatever it is you said you were doing."

I open my mouth to respond, but Liz ends the call before I get the chance. I shake my head as I stare at the receiver, worried for the man who dares to try to tie her down.

I glance at the clock again and let out a loud groan as I shove my face into the pillow. Liz's call reminded me of Ethan's and my expiration date, and now I'm debating whether it's a good idea to keep seeing him. Whether I want to admit it, I know I'm quickly becoming more attached to him than I have to any other man I've known. It terrifies me, and I'm definitely not ready to go through another heartache so soon after the situation with Tom.

Just as I decide I'm going to cancel, the door to my room slams open. I let out a screech, grabbing a pillow and holding it over my head like a weapon as I turn toward the intruder.

"I'm honestly curious what you plan to do with that."

Ethan smirks behind his usual mess of hair as he stands in the doorway, his massive frame taking up the entire space. Clutching the pillow to my chest, I send him a glare as he closes the door softly behind him.

"You know knocking is a thing, right?"

He chuckles under his breath. "Oh yes. But then I wouldn't get to see your reaction, would I?"

His voice sends a shiver down my spine, and I have to turn away so he can't see the effect he's having on me. Ethan's hand grips my chin, and I gasp, not even realizing he had made his way to the bed so quickly.

"You're so beautiful when you're frightened," he whispers, grinning down at me with a wicked glint in his dark irises. Sliding his hand around to the back of my neck, he holds me roughly in place while he crashes his lips down on mine. I moan against his mouth, feeling his hand tighten around my neck as I try to take over.

A low growl sounds from deep in his chest, and he nips my bottom lip, causing me to cry out in pain as he rears back to look at me. His cock twitches at the sound, and I watch his pupils blow before he leans down to kiss me again. Nursing the area he bit with his tongue, he trails a hand up my inner thigh, stopping just before he reaches my core. I whimper into his mouth, wriggling my hips down in a desperate attempt to make contact.

Ethan chuckles, letting his fingertips lightly brush against my pussy before pulling away completely. This time, I cry out in dismay, my lip pushed out in a deep pout as he adjusts himself in his jeans.

"We better get going, don't you think?"

I stare up at him in confusion, my mind still fuzzy from his touch.

"What? I told you I was starving." He grins down at me knowingly. "Ohhhh, did you think...? *Freckles,* you dirty girl."

"Shut up," I groan, crossing my arms over my chest in a deeper pout. "You suck."

"Actually, I think that's your forte, sweetheart."

"How original," I deadpan, sending him a glare. Ethan bellows a laugh, and I'm struck again by how handsome he looks when he smiles.

Dammit. Can't even stay mad at the bastard anymore.

"Where are we going? Or is it another surprise?" I ask, throwing my legs over the side of the mattress.

"The Sandbar. Nothing fancy—just good food, drinks, and music," he answers, looking like he regrets his decision already. "Throw on something comfy, and I'll meet you downstairs."

"Wait, why are you leaving?" I call after him, utterly confused as to why he's in such a hurry to escape the room.

He pauses, sighing with his hand on the doorknob. "I'm a strong man, Freckles. But if I have to stand here and watch you get undressed, we'll never leave this room. And I really am starving," he adds with a wink over his shoulder.

The Sandbar is a cute little bar with vintage beach souvenirs lining every nook and cranny of the weathered structure. The place is packed for a Thursday night, and I doubt we'll be able to squeeze our way up to the bar.

"Hey! John!" Ethan waves his hand in the air, and I follow his line of sight to the back of the bar. A bearded man in his forties stands behind the counter, well over seven feet tall and wide enough to be a linebacker. As soon as he spots the source calling his name, a cheerful grin lights up his intimidating features.

"Stone! Get your ass back here!" he bellows, motioning for the crowd to part with his massive arms. To my utter surprise, they do, and we easily make our way up to the front of the line.

"So this is the girl you won't shut up about." The man sends a wink in my direction. "Now I get what all the fuss is about."

"John, this is Amelia. Freckles, this is my buddy John," Ethan introduces us with a sigh. "One I thought was supposed to be off tonight."

"Aw, you're not tryin' to hide me from your lady,

are you?" John's belly shakes with a laugh as he reaches behind him for a bottle of Jack.

"Shit, why would I ever do that?" Ethan's voice drips with sarcasm as he accepts the shot glass John places in front of him.

John shrugs. "Who knows? I'm a catch."

Ethan chokes on his shot, and I giggle, causing John to turn to me with a grin.

"See? I knew I liked her," John coos, giving me a once-over.

"Watch it," Ethan growls, sending John a warning glance when his gaze lingers a tad too long on my chest. He reaches over and rests his hand on my hip possessively before pulling me tight against his side, and my face heats.

"Down, boy." John chuckles nervously, holding his hands up in a defensive stance. "What can I get you to drink, doll?"

"Tequila, if you don't mind." I grin timidly.

"Be right back," he says with a wink, then turns to grab the bottle.

"Sorry about John," Ethan murmurs against my ear. "He's harmless, just can't help himself around women as beautiful as you."

He nips my neck just below my earlobe, and I let out a sharp hiss as I crane my neck to the side to give him more access.

“Now you’re just rubbing it in my face.” John's teasing baritone brings me back to reality, and I instinctively try to put some space between us. Ethan’s strong arms hold me in place as I try to wriggle free, his chest shaking against my back in a silent chuckle.

”No one said you had to look,” he fires back, his eyes shooting a dare in John's direction.

“Someone’s a little touchy tonight,” he mutters, sliding a shot of clear liquid to me. “Your drink, doll. On the house.”

Then he looks over at Ethan. “Not for your ugly mug. You hurt my feelings.”

Ethan rolls his eyes. “Put it on my tab, then.”

“*Put it on my tab,*” John mocks in a high-pitched voice, waving his hands in the air. “No ‘*sorry, John.*’ No ‘*thank you for always putting up with my grouchy ass.*’ Honestly, doll, you might have a better time with someone more like me.”

Ethan throws his head back in a laugh, but his grip tightens around my waist.

“Someone like what? An alcoholic lumberjack with a beer gut?”

“I’m *big-boned!*” John roars, but it looks like he’s trying to hold back a laugh. “And yes, actually.” He slaps a hand across his great stomach. “The ladies love it. Not everyone wants to cuddle with a bulldozer, Stone.”

Ethan rolls his eyes before turning his attention back to me, leaning his mouth back down to my neck and kissing the area gently.

"Can I get another shot? One for her, too. She'll need it after listening to you run your mouth for so long," Ethan growls. John huffs but does so with a grin toying at his mouth, and I can tell everything between the two is in good fun.

"Cheers to a wonderful night with a beautiful woman at my side." Ethan taps his cup against mine before taking it down in a single, effortless swallow. I follow suit, feeling the room sway as it burns down my throat.

"Ugh. Cheers." I cough, leaning my weight back against Ethan for support. He chuckles low in his throat and wraps his arms around me, leaning his cheek down to rest against my shoulder as he nuzzles my neck.

"As much as I want to stand here with your ass pressed against me, I have to go take a leak," Ethan whispers against my ear. My cheeks heat, and I step forward, only to be dragged back against his chest.

"I didn't say you could go yet." He hums, trailing a hand up my thigh and stopping at the hem of my shorts.

"I thought you had to pee?" I gulp as his fingers work their way past the fabric and dip inside me.

"What can I say? You're utterly addicting." He groans, leaning back much too soon. Spinning me around, he hungrily crashes his lips against mine, toying and nipping at my bottom lip before pulling away completely.

"Fuck," he whispers, pressing his forehead against mine. "You're going to be the death of me, I swear."

With a deep sigh, he backs away. "You gonna be okay by yourself for a few minutes?"

I nod, feeling butterflies roar to life in my belly with the way he's looking at me.

"Okay. Be right back, baby girl." Placing a quick peck on the tip of my nose, he turns and disappears into the crowd.

I sigh and gaze around the packed space, feeling suddenly cold and alone in his absence.

Get it together, girl. I'm leaving in a few days. I can't be pining after him like this. It'll just make everything worse when I have to go back home.

I shake my head to clear away the negative voice. Leaning my elbows against the bar top, I hang my head between my shoulders and hope Ethan returns soon so I can stop feeling this way.

"Hulloo."

The garbled voice in my ear makes me jump, and I spin around to face a man in his early thirties with thinning blond hair. The stranger's hazel eyes are dull and bloodshot from too much of whatever reeks on his breath, and the creepy smile he gives me sends a shiver down my spine.

"Um, hi," I murmur, looking around nervously for Ethan.

"Can I getchu a drink?" The man gives me a crooked smile, and I try to take a step back into the counter.

"No, thank you," I answer, hoping my voice is assertive enough to make him piss off. "My date's about to come back, so I think you should—"

"Comonnnn, let me buy you one." He slobbers, clearly not getting the hint by his stupid shit-eating grin.

"I said no thank you." I glare at him, then turn away so he finally gets it.

A loud *slap* is heard across the room, followed by a sharp sting as the stranger's palm connects with my ass. My eyes go wide in shock, and I turn back to face the man with a proud grin spread across his face.

"You like that, baby? There's more where that came from."

Too stunned to speak, I turn to John, whose face has drained to a shade of white.

"You're an unlucky sonofabitch, you know that?"

"Fuck are you talking about?" The man puffs out his chest, mistaking John's ashen expression for fear.

"Because normally, I would just kick your ass out of here. But now... now Stone is gonna fucking kill you."

"Man, fuck you. Who the hell even is that?"

Before anyone can say another word, Ethan's fist flies through the air, connecting with the side of the man's jaw in a sickening *crack!*

Chapter Fifteen

I scream as the stranger's body falls to the floor in a limp heap, the scene before me playing out in slow motion.

"She said no," Ethan growls, cracking his knuckles together as he towers over him. Just now regaining consciousness, he blinks slowly up at Ethan's murderous frame. Either too stupid or too drunk to realize the trouble he was in, the man tries to pick himself off the floor.

"Fuck is your problem, dude?" he growls, raising a hand to massage his swollen jaw. "Go find some other slut to play white knight with. This one's mine."

Before I have time to react, the man grabs me by the back of the head, weaving his fingers into my hair and pulling hard. I yelp, feeling like my scalp is on fire as he yanks my head into his chest. I push my palms against his abdomen in an attempt to get away, but he holds me tight with the strength of the testosterone-fueled moron he is.

"Let go of me, fucker!" I hiss, struggling uselessly against his grip.

"Relax, babe." He leans down to brush his nose against my neck. "He's not gonna do anyth–*oomph!*"

I stumble back as the man's limbs are ripped from my body. By the time I regain my balance, a crowd has already formed a circle around the two, completely blocking my line of sight.

"Ethan!" I scream, hearing the horrifying crunch of bone against bone ring out through the space. "Ethan, stop! You'll kill him!"

Hearing the blows picking up speed, I squeeze through the throng of bodies and feel my stomach lurch at the sight. Three fully grown men have leaped onto Ethan in an attempt to subdue him, which only seems to have added fuel to his fire.

"Ethan, please!" I scream over the roaring and gasps of the crowd. "Ethan, you need to stop!"

As I choke on the panic swelling in my throat, my cries fall on deaf ears, and I know there's only one way I can get him to stop. Not giving myself time to think about all the ways this could go horribly wrong, I run right into the line of fire. As soon as Ethan reels back for another punch, I jump between the two, wrapping my arms and legs around his torso like a koala.

Ethan stops, his muscles frozen in place as I lower my lips to his ear.

"Ethan, please. You need to stop this," I whisper, digging my fingernails into his back as his breath picks up speed. "Please. You've done enough."

"No." His voice hitches in his throat. "He hasn't learned his lesson yet."

"Please," I beg, sliding my fingers gently across his back. "For me?"

Ethan takes a deep breath before blowing it out of his nose. A second later, he shoves me off him and makes a motion to stand.

With fire in his dark irises, he glares down at me. "You shouldn't have stopped me."

"You would have killed him if I didn't!"

"So you just throw all self-preservation out the window? Why the fuck do you even care so much about this asshole?"

I drag my eyes down to my shoes, feeling my face heat with embarrassment.

"It's not him I care about."

Ethan holds a hand up to his ear. "I'm sorry, what was that?"

"I said it's not *him* who I care about!" I practically scream in his face, feeling my eyes well up with unshed tears. *God, this isn't how I wanted to have this conversation.*

"Stone! Cops are on the way!" John bellows.

Ethan doesn't seem to hear him as he stares murderously down at the stranger, his fist twitching at his side like he's seconds away from jumping him again.

John gives me a desperate look and hooks his thumb in the direction of the exit. "You gotta get him out of here, doll. *Now.*"

I look back and forth between the men helplessly, not quite sure what I'm supposed to do.

"Hey! It's Amelia, right?"

Wordlessly, I nod in John's direction.

"Look, Amelia. The cops will be here any minute, and you really don't want Ethan to be around when they show. You're the only one he'll listen to, so *please*, get him out."

Watching the bearded, seven-foot behemoth of a man beg me for help seems to snap me out of my trance, and I spring into action.

"Ethan." I say his name softly, the muscles in his back rippling as I place my hand against his skin. "Ethan, I need you to get me out of here. Please?"

At my plea, he whips his head toward me, his dark eyes softening as he takes in my expression.

"Okay."

To my surprise, he takes me gruffly by the hand and starts dragging me toward the exit, the sound of our footsteps ringing out loudly in the stunned silence. We make our way silently down the wooden steps, Ethan guiding me by my arm protectively the whole way.

Our footsteps shuffle across the crosswalk and down the sidewalk toward the hotel, the avenue empty with only a few streetlamps around to illuminate our way.

Lost in thought, I don't pay attention to where I'm stepping, and the tip of my sneaker snags a loose paver, sending my body crashing down to the sidewalk in front of me. I close my eyes, bracing for the impact that never comes.

I look back to see Ethan wearing a bemused smirk as he holds me midair between his two strong palms. His fingertips tighten around my waist as he hoists me upright and back into his chest before flipping me around to face him.

"Are you okay?" he asks, his eyes searching my face for any signs of discomfort.

I nod wordlessly.

"Are you sure?" he asks, gently gripping my jaw and guiding my face up to meet him. The brooding intensity pouring from his gaze leaves my legs feeling numb, and I lean farther into his embrace to steady myself.

"I'm okay," I squeak. Seeing the corners of his mouth begin to make their way into a frown, I add, "I just feel a little silly, that's all."

"That's not what I mean, and you know it," He looks down at me, his eyes dark and foreboding.

"I promise." I swear, looking up into his eyes daringly. "It's not like I haven't had my ass smacked by some drunk before."

My words have the opposite effect I intended. Instead of laughing, Ethan's eyes darken, and he scowls, pulling me flush against his chest as he lets out a low, animalistic growl.

"I should've killed the fuck," he mutters, digging his fingertips into my shoulder blades and pulling me even closer against him. "I would have, if you hadn't stopped me."

"I'm glad you didn't. I would have missed you in prison."

My stomach knots with lust pinned beneath his brooding gaze, and I bury my face into his chest to hide the heat rising in my cheeks. Ethan loosens his bear-like grip, taking his index finger and forcing my chin up, daring my eyes to meet his.

"I would never let anything bad happen to you," he continues, his voice a low hum in the dim light of the streetlamp. "Even if it means prison time. It scares me, the things I would do for you."

My blush deepens, and I let out a nervous chuckle, trying hopelessly to escape the intensity of his gaze. He slides his hand up to cup my face, stroking my cheek with his thumb and pulling back slightly to press his lips against my cheek.

"You're precious, Amelia. You deserve to be protected," he breathes out against my ear.

After a few moments of silence, his grip loosens, and I jut my chin up, exposing my face fully to the cheap fluorescent lighting. He closes his eyes and groans, raking his fingernails up the base of my neck and grabbing a fistful of hair before giving it a gentle tug to the right, allowing access to the side of my neck.

"And God, are you beautiful," he whispers, using his teeth to nip the base of my earlobe, then to continue the sequence down my neck.

Goose bumps run up my spine as Ethan rakes his teeth against my exposed skin, using his mouth to gently suck the area directly below my ear. I let out a low moan, unconsciously tipping my head to the side and offering him easier access as he works his way south, leaving tiny trails of fire everywhere his lips touch.

"God, I need you," he groans desperately, yanking the edge of my blouse below my shoulder and resuming his stream of delicate kisses across my collarbone.

With a look I can only describe as hungry, Ethan grabs my waist and whirls me up against the light post. Swooping down and pressing his lips hard against my mouth, desire starts to burn its way across every inch of my skin, and I open my lips for him. My core burns with want, and I have to fight the urge to let him take me right here, exposed to anyone and everything.

As if reading my mind, Ethan uses the hand anchoring my hip to swing my body around and presses my ass back against his bulge. With his free hand, he weaves his fingers up the nape of my neck and grabs a fistful of my messy red locks, using his leverage to pull my head back against his chest. Now that I'm pinned, he slides his free hand around my windpipe, successfully trapping me between him and the post.

Fuck, are we really doing this? Here?

Before I can form another thought, Ethan's fingers begin dancing rapidly beneath my shorts, and I gasp, all logical thought leaving my mind as he toys with the edges of my thong.

Keeping me entrapped in the violent embrace, Ethan presses his lips against my neck, feeling the rapid rise and fall of my chest against his forearm.

"You're mine," he growls. "Aren't you?"

Feeling my frantic, speechless nodding, Ethan lets

out a low chuckle, the sound reverberating in his chest against the back of my head.

"It's almost unfair how beautiful you are. The way you make me feel…" He trails off, reaching underneath my blouse and rolling my nipple between his thumb and index finger.

"Fuck, I need you," he groans.

Stopping his work to take my whole breast in his palm, he tightens his grip, leaning in to kiss my ear.

"So I'm going to have you."

Abruptly letting go of my throat, Ethan presses his palm between my shoulder blades and shoves me forward into the post. I feel the cool metallic finish beneath my palms as I brace myself, hearing the familiar click of his belt unbuckling behind me.

Ethan grasps both sides of my hips before reaching around to unbutton my shorts.

"Right now."

My entire being burning with his promise, he yanks my shorts down to my ankles, and I let out a small gasp as he presses his cock against my ass. Holding himself with one arm, he reaches down and trails his fingernails up the inside of my thigh, pushing the tip of his thumb inside my dripping cunt.

I gasp, arching back against him as Ethan lets out a low chuckle against my neck.

"Something tells me," he grumbles, slipping his

thumb out to tease it against my clit, "you wouldn't mind that one bit."

He pulls his fingers away and, hearing me whimper, lets out another all-knowing chuckle. Ethan starts rubbing the tip of his cock back and forth across my clit, and I can't help but cry out in desperation.

Just when I think I'll explode from the desire building in my core, Ethan pauses, grabs both of my hips, and shoves his cock deep inside me.

"Oh fuck!" I moan, using my hands to steady myself against the slim post as Ethan plows into me again and again, the rest of the world fading away the harder he fucks me.

"You're mine," he growls, reaching around with one hand and encircling my throat, applying light pressure to stop the oxygen flow to my head. My eyes roll to the back of my head in bliss, feeling the slip of unconsciousness as he tightens his hold around my windpipe.

"Mine," he growls.

With one final thrust, my walls tighten around his cock, and I let out a scream as I come, my legs quaking and barely able to keep me upright.

After a few more thrusts, Ethan follows suit, his thick cock throbbing deep inside me with his release. Letting out a moan, he collapses on my back, bracing his arms against the pole as he starts flooding out of me.

Ethan straightens up with a groan, steadying my trembling frame in front of him. He pulls his palm back without warning and delivers a single stinging blow to my bare ass cheek.

I yelp at the sensation, whimpering and attempting to wriggle away as the heat rises where Ethan had struck my sensitive skin.

He appeases me by massaging the area, gently kneading and caressing the bright-pink handprint before reaching down and pulling my shorts up again. Ethan quickly follows suit, pulling his slim-fit denim back up and securing them around his waist with his belt.

With a final *zip,* his hand lands on my shoulder, and I'm whirled around to face him. Ethan reaches up, cupping my face lovingly and using his thumb to trace delicate circles across the apple of my cheek.

When he dips his forehead down to rest gently on mine, I close my eyes and smile, feeling safe and warm in his embrace despite the short time I've known him. I look up at him, doe-eyed and anxious, before burying my face against his chest in embarrassment.

Ethan chuckles, smoothing the back of my hair with his palm.

"That's my girl," he croons, kissing the crown of

my head and encircling me in his arms. With my head nestled perfectly in the crook of his shoulder, I relax against him, allowing the feeling of safety to wash over me. He holds me in the dusk for a while, caressing my body tenderly with adoration dancing in his eyes at every whimper his touch springs from me.

Nearly collapsing against him in bliss, my eyes shoot wide open as his cum leaks out of me. Feeling me freeze, Ethan pulls back with a devilish smile, a look of mock concern plastered across his face as I wiggle my thighs together.

Still grinning, he snakes his hand up my neck, stopping at my jaw to flick his thumb across my swollen lips.

"I'm sorry, I couldn't help myself. I just *really* needed to be inside you." His voice is a low, dangerous rumble as he adds, "Plus, you look *so* beautiful with my cum dripping out of you."

I gulp, my eyes widening as I squirm in his embrace. Keeping me firmly trapped against him, he gives me another kiss on my forehead.

"Come on." He drops his arms and steps back, his eyes dark and full of amusement. "The night is still young, and I want to show you something."

Chapter Sixteen

We walk in comfortable silence for some time, listening to the cicadas chirp as we shuffle across the empty boardwalk toward the tip of the island. We left the last of civilization behind long ago, and only the light of the moon illuminates our path through the mangrove forest.

"We're almost there," Ethan murmurs, sensing my restlessness.

"I trust you," I return. "Although, if you planned to turn into an axe murderer, this is the perfect spot to do it."

"How brave of you." Ethan laughs, fitting his fingers in mine and giving my hand a light squeeze.

"Eh, not really. I have my sources that say you're a pretty good dude."

"Oh?" He turns to me with a lifted brow. "And

who would that be? I can't have my reputation ruined with those kinds of rumors floating around."

"Your sister, for one. She seems to think you're a really great guy or something crazy like that."

Ethan shakes his head with a chuckle. "Cass said that? Now I know you're fucking with me."

"Am not!" I stick my tongue out at him. "And nothing is wrong with being a good man, Ethan."

"Yeah, well," Ethan says, a tinge of bitterness in his voice, "it makes it a whole lot easier for people to take advantage of you, that's for sure."

As soon as the words leave his mouth, Ethan turns his head away. I only see a flash of emotion, but it's enough to make my heart ache, thinking of all the reasons behind the hurt in his beautiful brown eyes.

"Do you wanna talk about it?" I ask, making sure to keep my voice soft so he doesn't spook.

"Sure, if you want me to ruin the mood." His laughter holds no amusement, only bitterness.

I stop short, causing him to look back at me in surprise.

"What if I want to know more about you? Would that be ruining the mood?"

"Look, just..." He pauses, rubbing a hand across his face gruffly. "I'll tell you whatever you wanna know, but we have to keep moving while I do. Deal?"

"Deal." I grin happily and start up the pace from

before. "Cassandra told me you had trust issues. Care to spill the reason?"

Ethan lets out a cold laugh. "Of *course* she did."

"That doesn't sound like an answer, mister."

He shoots me a look out of the corner of his eye, and I have to suppress a giggle.

"Come on. If you do it fast, it'll be like ripping off a Band-Aid."

"You make such compelling arguments, Freckles. You really missed your calling as a lawyer."

"You're stalling," I groan, looking back up at him with a pout. "If it's mommy issues, you can just say that."

"Jesus." Ethan bellows, looking over at me with shock in his eyes. "You really just go right in, don't you?"

"Are you trying to say that I'm right?"

"Sure." He sighs again, running a hand through his hair. "You can say that."

"And what would you say?" I ask, determined more than ever to get the story.

"I'd say that my childhood was fucked, and my mother and father can burn in hell," he growls, his brow coming together at whatever memory swirls in his mind. Shaking his head, he goes quiet for a minute before elaborating.

"Our mom left when I was a teenager. Cass was

just a baby, and our dad was too fucking wasted all the time to get his piss in the toilet, much less take care of a newborn. So that left me."

I squeeze his hand for reassurance, and his lips lift into a small smile before instantly being replaced by the tortured expression from earlier.

"The most fucked-up part wasn't even that she left. It wasn't that I had to drop out of high school to pay the bills, or that I could never go to med school like I had dreamed...it's the fact that she started a whole new family almost immediately after ditching us. She even had the nerve to send a Christmas card or two, if you can believe it."

I stop again, causing my hand to slip from his as he carries on a few more steps. Confused, he turns back to face me, and I throw my arms around his neck and bury my face there.

"I'm so sorry, Ethan," I murmur, my voice hoarse with unshed tears. "You didn't deserve any of that, it... it's fucking unspeakable."

"What's all this, Freckles?" he asks, running his hands softly across my back. "You going soft on me? Where's that fiery attitude I love so much?"

I swat his shoulder playfully. "Shut up. I'm trying to comfort you."

"Why? My life turned out pretty fucking great." He pulls back to give me one of his patented smirks before placing his lips on the top of my head. "Plus, I don't think I was ever meant to work with people that closely. I'd probably snap and pull a scalpel on someone, you know?"

I giggle into his chest, feeling my eyes dry the longer he embraces me.

"You do have quite the temper."

His chest shakes with a chuckle. "Only for you, sweetheart." He swats my ass lightly with his palm. "Come on, now. I'd like to get there sometime tonight."

Holding his hand out for me, Ethan leads us to the edge of the boardwalk and steps off the side, motioning for me to duck my head as he squeezes through a small break in the tree line. Wild mangroves almost completely cover the path in all directions, and I have to travel directly behind Ethan to fit through the tunnel-like space.

As soon as we step out into the clearing, I gasp. A small, secluded inlet lay before us, cut off from view by the thick tree line and towering cliffs on either side. The beach looks luminescent in the moonlight, with some of the softest white sands I've ever seen.

"Beautiful, isn't it?" Ethan whispers, coming up behind me to wrap his arms around my waist. "Only the locals know about this place. That's why it looks like this—untouched. Perfect."

"It really is," I murmur, mesmerized by the layers of moonlight dancing across the top of the crystal-clear water.

"I've, uh... never taken anyone here before," he confesses, his voice raw with emotion. "No one ever really seemed special enough before."

Feeling like fireworks are going off in my belly, I whip around to face him, my eyes wide and glowing in the dusk.

"Amelia...I've never met anyone like you before. You're..." He stops, his dark irises wrought with intensity. "God, you're just so *beautiful,*" He moans, pulling me into him hard and kissing me.

"Ethan," I moan as he begins kissing down my neck. "I don't ever want to stop feeling like this."

"You don't have to, love," he whispers, nipping my ear lightly and sending goose bumps running down the back of my neck. "Not while I'm around."

Expertly lowering us onto the sand bed, Ethan cups my face in his palm, staring down at me adoringly as he spreads my legs and wraps them around his waist.

"You're mine, aren't you?" Ethan questions, his eyes burning with lust as he pushes my shorts over my hips.

He trails his hand up my thigh until his fingertips lightly brush my core, and I gasp, pressing my full breasts up into him with a moan.

"Yes! Yes, please," I beg as he rubs the tip of his cock teasingly across my slit.

"Since you said please," he murmurs, sliding his full length into me with a loud, guttural moan.

Leaning down over me, he presses his lips against my ear, breathing out deeply as he thrusts in and out of me.

"I can make you feel like this every night if you let me."

Lost in utter pleasure and bliss, I simply nod, unable to think of a single thing in the world I would want more than this, more than him.

Utterly exhausted from last night, I roll into Ethan's side and fall back asleep, far more concerned with a few more minutes of slumber than the fact that I have to be up and ready to go to Cass's party in an hour. We returned to my room around midnight last night but didn't fall asleep until the early morning hours. My body ached from being used so many times, but I was more content than ever. In my opinion, it's a fair price to pay for a few hours of missed sleep.

When my eyes open for the second time, Ethan is no longer beside me in bed. There is, however, a sticky note on the pillow.

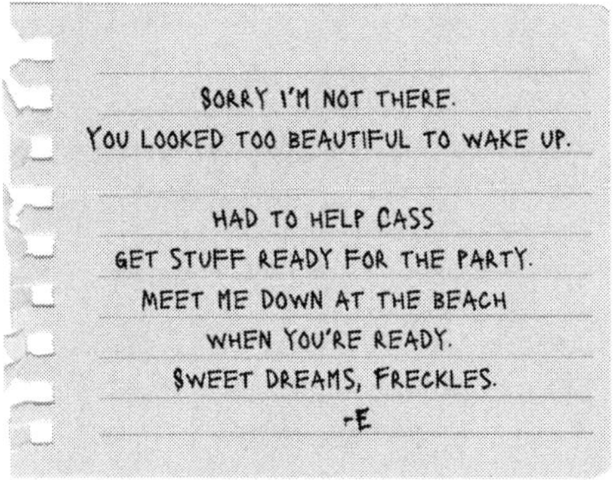

SORRY I'M NOT THERE.
YOU LOOKED TOO BEAUTIFUL TO WAKE UP.

HAD TO HELP CASS
GET STUFF READY FOR THE PARTY.
MEET ME DOWN AT THE BEACH
WHEN YOU'RE READY.
SWEET DREAMS, FRECKLES.
-E

Looking at the space next to me, I feel an unusual pang of sadness in my chest, and I can't help wondering what will happen tomorrow when waking up alone is once again the norm.

My eyes burn with unshed tears as I think of the last day I have left in Pebble Beach, of Ethan. What's going to happen to us when I go home to Chicago? When the wonder of this whole thing wears off, and we're just two people who live thousands of miles apart?

I shake my head, bewildered at the intrusive thoughts and sheer dread they bring. I don't want to think about leaving—not now. Not after the night Ethan and I had just shared, baring our souls to each other and talking through the night like long-lost friends.

Resolving to deal with my worries later, I push all

my fear and anxiety to the back of my mind and focus instead on what I'll wear to the party. Settling on one of my favorite light-blue bikinis, I throw on a pair of cutoffs and flip-flops, and head down to the beach. As soon as I spot the boat, I begin shuffling quicker across the white-hot sand, desperate to locate Ethan. I'm certain some of the uneasiness stuck with me all morning will dissipate when I'm in his arms again, and I don't want to wait a minute longer.

"Morning, sleepyhead," Ethan calls across the distance. As I get closer, I notice he unashamedly runs his eyes up and down my bikini-clad frame. Throwing his muscular arms around me in his signature embrace, he presses his lips against my neck.

"I missed you," he whispers, just loud enough for me to hear.

"It's only been a few hours, silly," I quip, though my pulse races at his confession.

"And that means I can't miss you? Since when?" He pulls back to smirk down at me.

"Touché," I mumble, pressing my face back into his chest.

"Well?"

"Well, what?"

"Aren't you going to say you missed me too?" His tone is teasing, but something about his demeanor tells a different story.

"I... Of course I missed you."

Something like relief flashes across his face at my words before his usual confident smile returns.

"Amelia Hayes, is that a blush I see?"

I roll my eyes, feeling my cheeks redden for real.

"So what if it is?"

"It's cute, is what it is," Ethan mutters, pulling me into a kiss. I let out a sigh as his tongue works its way across my lips, grateful for his strong hold on my waist as my knees start to shake.

Ethan pulls back, his expression utterly serious as he furrows his thick brows. "I'm sorry I wasn't there when you woke up this morning. You got my note, right?"

Though his intense gaze never lets up, I swear I can see the slightest tinge of pink spread across his cheeks.

Knowing mine are at least twice as bright, I nuzzle my head back against his chest.

"I did. I thought it was adorable."

"Yeah, yeah. I can't believe what a simp you're turning me into, either." Ethan laughs, squeezing me even tighter against him.

"Did you just say simp?" I ask, my voice teasing.

"I like to keep up with the lingo. What's wrong with that?" he shoots back, equally as amused.

I giggle, jumping up and wrapping myself around him like a koala.

"You're too cute." I grin brightly as I kiss the tip of his nose.

"Mmm. Says the fluffy bunny rabbit."

"Excuse me?" I balk at him. "What the hell is that supposed to mean?"

"What?" He laughs, holding a hand up in mock defense. "I just happen to think you're adorable."

"Adorable, huh?".

"Adorable, cute, pretty...ungodly sexy." He trails his hand over the curves of my body. "You really do have it all."

His voice now a low, hungry growl, I freeze in his arms, feeling goose bumps run down the length of my spine.

"We should probably join the rest of the party?" I gulp, everything in my body screaming to stay right where we are, no matter who's waiting for us.

A reminder of the party seems to snap Ethan out of whatever is going through his mind. Letting out a dramatic groan, he concedes.

"Yeah, you're right. I don't trust them to leave without us."

I try to lower myself back to the ground, but I'm held in place by Ethan's unrelenting grip. He leans his lips down to my ear, and his voice comes out in a soft growl. "Don't think you're getting off later, Freckles. Teasing me all day dressed in *this.*" He pauses to run his thumb across my thin bikini strap, sending shivers down the nape of my neck. "It's almost as if you're *begging* me to take you right here and now."

"What? I'm not—" I sputter, my cheeks flaming red as I stare wide-eyed up at him.

"I'm just *teasing.*" He deftly flicks his thumb across my bottom lip as he inches his face closer to mine. Reflexively, I jut my chin up to meet him, closing my eyes as I wait for the kiss that never comes.

Feeling my feet connect with the hot sand, I open my eyes to see Ethan already several paces toward the water.

"Wha—Ethan!" I cry, my mouth hanging open as I watch him stalk away.

"See what I mean? *Teasing.*" He whips around, hunching over in laughter at the look on my face.

"Are you coming or what?"

I pause, a mischievous twinkle in my eye before bursting out, "That's what she said!"

He shakes his head with a chuckle.

"Race you back, slowpoke!" I call, running past him at a full sprint.

Chapter Seventeen

When we make it to the shoreline, puffing and exhausted from the race, I look up and see Cass waving at me from the back of a motorboat.

"You guys made it! Hop on in. We're about to take off!"

"You heard the boss." Ethan takes my hand and leads me through the water to the boat. He hoists me over the side with ease, letting his hand linger on my ass a little longer than necessary before following me.

"I'm *so* glad you're here!" Cass exclaims, throwing her arms around me in a vise-like grip. "There's way too much testosterone on this boat for my liking."

I chuckle while trying to wiggle free, looking at Ethan for assistance. He just smirks, holding his hands up in a helpless gesture.

"Don't look at me. I'm part of the problem, remember?"

"You sure as shit are!" Cass wrinkles her nose at her brother before turning her attention back to me. "I may need you to run interference if you don't mind. I kind of invited..." She pauses, sneaking a peek at Ethan out of the corner of her eye.

"A boy," she whispers, waggling her brows at me suggestively. "Basically, I just need you to distract Ethan today, which shouldn't be a problem because you do that naturally."

"What are you whispering about?" Ethan questions, crossing his arms over his chest with a pointed look in her direction.

"It's girl stuff." Cass rolls her eyes. "You wouldn't get it."

"Like hell I wouldn't!"

"Ethan," I coo, turning to run my hand down his arm, "it's okay, I promise. You don't need to be worried about anything."

He turns to me, his eyes softening as he scans the sincerity on my face.

"Nope. I still don't trust her," he deadpans, turning to send Cass a glare. "It's about a boy, isn't it?"

Cass rolls her eyes. "You know I'm twenty-two, right?"

"I don't see what that has to do with anything."

She sighs, turning to me with a groan. "You see why I needed you here today?"

I giggle into my hand but stop short when I notice Ethan's furious expression. Like an angel sent from above, Jace's voice breaks the awkward silence between us.

"What's going on, guys?"

Ethan whips his head in Jace's direction, watching for a moment as he hauls himself over the side of the boat.

"Did you know she was seeing someone?" Ethan questions, his voice low and deadly.

"Who, Marcus?" Jace shrugs as he makes his way over to the wheel. "I guess you could call it that."

"And you're *okay* with this?"

Jace freezes, his eyes flashing with a warning only Ethan and I catch. "Yeah, man. Why wouldn't I be?"

Ethan huffs, rolling his eyes to the sky. "Fucking pussy," he mutters.

"Okay, is something going on that I should know about?" Cass pipes up, calling our attention back to her. "Because it really seems that way."

"Hey! Sorry I'm late, Cass, I had to pick up—okay, what did I miss?"

We all whip around to face the new addition, breathing a sigh of relief as Cass seems to forget her earlier question.

"Marcus!" she squeals, running over to the side of the boat and grabbing the pack of seltzers from his lanky arms. "You got my favorite!"

Marcus looks among all our faces, seeming a little spooked from whatever he just walked in on.

"So, uh...everything's cool? Because it kinda seemed like—"

"Everything is fine, *Marcus.*" Ethan interrupts, his voice dripping venom. "Why don't you make yourself at home? Here, you can sit right next to me."

Cass shoots me a pained look, and I reach over to grab Ethan's arm. At my touch, he jumps, but I watch his expression soften as he looks at where my hand lies. Pulling me into his chest, he lowers his head down to my neck, letting out a deep sigh of satisfaction as he breathes me in.

"How do you do that?" he murmurs, kissing my cheek delicately.

My brows draw together. "Do what?"

"Make the rest of the world go away." He sighs, crushing me further into his chest. "I've never been able to do that. Not until you came along."

My heart swells with his words, and I turn my head to place a kiss on his cheek.

"Get a room, assholes!"

Ethan whips his head toward Marcus while I try to hide my reddening face in his chest.

"What the fuck did you just say?" Ethan asks, his voice unusually calm.

"Dude, chill. It was a joke." He laughs, clearly not noticing the horrified looks on everyone's faces. When no one joins in, he throws his hands in the air and scoffs.

"What's everyone's problem? It. Was. A. Jo—"

Before he can finish, Ethan steps forward and shoves at Marcus's chest, the force of it sending his body somersaulting over the side and into the water.

He resurfaces a moment later, sputtering and coughing up salt water.

"What the... What the fuck?" he screeches, looking over at Cassandra. "Your brother is a fucking psycho!"

"Relax. It was a joke," Ethan seethes, shooting Marcus a warning glance as he tries to haul himself up again.

"Cass? Are you really gonna let this fucker do this to me?"

"Um, first of all." Cass holds her index in the air and cocks her hip out to the side. "The only people allowed to diss my brother are me and Amelia. And *second...*" She pauses, sending him a death glare of her own. "You are officially uninvited to my birthday party. Start her up, Jace!"

Chuckling under his breath, he complies, turning the ignition so the engine roars to life.

"Toodle loo, asshole!" she calls, wiggling her fingertips at his stunned expression as we peel away from the shore. "Oh, and thanks for the seltzers!"

Ethan pulls me tight against his side, placing a kiss on my cheek with a chuckle. While Cass is distracted, he turns to Jace, lowering his voice so us three are the only ones who can hear.

"You owe me one."

Jace rolls his eyes but stays quiet, and I swear I see the faintest shade of pink color his cheeks. Ethan smirks down at me, shooting me a knowing look as Jace speeds across the open water.

"I'm sorry...breakneck?" I repeat, a hint of horror in my voice.

"Yeah." Cass shrugs casually and continues her pace across the sand. "It's the giant cliff that faces the cove. The tallest jump-off point is probably... fifty feet high? Give or take."

"Give or take," I mumble, my fight-or-flight response kicking in and pushing heavily for the latter.

"Hey, guys?" I look over at Cass, but the excitement in her eyes causes my protest to get caught in my throat.

"Yeah, what's up?"

"Uh, nothing. Never mind." I give her a smile, but I have a feeling it comes out more like a grimace. "Just wondering how far we have to walk to get to this... breakneck."

With a grin, Cass gestures to a thick swath of Australian pines just past the beachline.

"There's a little clearing through there. We follow the path for a half mile or so, and we're there."

"Awesome." I sigh and reach for Ethan's arm. His muscles ripple under my touch, and I smile as some of my anxiety melts away.

As we get closer to our destination, I begin to notice how familiar my surroundings seem. The scent of pine tar and salt fills my senses, and I'm taken back to the time, many years ago, when I took this same path with my mom. It's almost eerie how similar everything is, from the slim footworn path to the sound of the trees creaking in the stillness.

Closing my eyes, I grip Ethan tighter and lose myself in the nostalgia, allowing him to lead me blindly for the rest of the way.

"We're here, beautiful," Ethan whispers, stopping short and freeing me from my trance. Peeking through the last of the shrubbery blocking my view, I gasp.

A circular pool of crystal-clear water lies below us, surrounded by massive, rocky cliffs. A small tunnel leads out to the ocean, providing water flow into the cove while hiding the place from the outside. A thick rope tied to one of the pines disappears over the edge of the cliff, and I have a sinking realization that we'll be using it to shimmy back up out of the water.

With this thought, I turn to Ethan, my eyes wide with fright.

"Oh, come on now. Don't give me that look."

"What look?" I stick my lip out toward him.

"That one. The one where you pretend you're too scared to do anything adventurous. You saved a turtle from shark-infested waters, for fuck's sake. This jump will be a piece of cake for you."

"Oh shit. You knew about the sharks?" The blood drains from Jace's face as he looks between Ethan and me.

"Your dad mentioned it." He shoots Jace a deadly glance. "And I want you to know that if anything had happened to her, you would be a dead man."

Jace gulps audibly, eliciting a giggle from Cass as Ethan turns his attention back to me.

"Freckles," he murmurs, reaching over to grip my chin lightly, "you know I'd never let anything bad happen to you, don't you?"

The intensity in his voice makes me gulp like Jace, causing Ethan to break character as he hunches over in laughter.

"Did I ever tell you that you're fucking adorable?"

“Eh, once or twice.” I grin, leaning over to peck his cheek. “But I never mind hearing it again.”

“Oh, I bet you don’t.” He chuckles, leading me slowly toward the ledge. I stop a few feet from the drop, peering over the edge with my heart thrumming wildly in my chest. Suddenly, I’m reminded of the terror I felt that day my mom took me out here; how I looked down into the abyss and felt fear take over, freezing my body in place no matter how much I wanted to jump off with everyone else.

Sensing my apprehension, Ethan wraps his arm around my waist and gives me a reassuring squeeze.

“Come on, girl!” Cass hollers from atop Jace’s shoulders. “You got this shit!”

Jace chuckles, calling equally as loudly, “What she said!”

I double over in laughter, thankful that some of my previous nerves are melting away. Catching my breath, I straighten up and grab Ethan’s hand as I face the edge once more.

“You ready?” Ethan looks down at me, the gentle expression telling me that he would never force me into something I’m not comfortable with.

With newfound adrenaline coursing through my veins, I jut my chin up proudly.

“You betcha.” My voice sounds a hell of a lot more confident than I’m feeling.

"That's my *girl!*" Ethan whoops excitedly, grabbing me by the waist and hoisting me into the air. He places me gently back on the ground before smacking my ass to give me a jolt.

"Here I gooooo!" I giggle, charging full speed toward the great abyss. As soon as my feet leave the safety of the ground, my body goes *oh, fuck no,* and a piercing scream rips from my throat. I flail in the air, but gravity is a bitch, and I plummet to the water below against my wishes.

Ethan yells a battle cry somewhere above me, obviously having the time of his life. The farther I fall, the freer I feel, and I let go for the first time in my life. I have just enough time to fill my lungs with a breath before my body makes contact with the water, and I plunge into the icy abyss. The briny water fills my nose and mouth as my head shoots underwater, and I struggle to kick to the surface, grateful for the little oxygen I was able to get before I went down.

"Beautiful? You okay?" I hear Ethan splashing frantically toward me between my coughing fits, but I'm too busy trying to get the saltwater out of my lungs to answer right away.

Ethan wraps his arms around me protectively, expertly keeping us both afloat by swinging his strong legs back and forth beneath us. His eyes scan my face with worry, looking for any signs of injury.

"That...was *awesome.*"

At my words, all the concern wipes clean from his expression. He relaxes his grip as a huge, cheesy smile spreads across his face.

"Do you wanna go again?"

"Hells yeah!" I yell out excitedly, slapping my palm over my mouth after the outburst.

Ethan lets out a booming laugh, looking deep into my eyes with an intensity I've never seen before. Before long, he breaks away, ushering me to swim back with him to the edge.

Chapter Eighteen

YESTERDAY FLEW BY IN A WHIRLWIND OF SUN, sand, laughter, and great company. As much as I tried, I couldn't quite bring myself to tell him I was leaving the next day. In truth, I didn't want to think about it. I didn't want to imagine what life would be like without him.

Today is that day, and I'm no more ready to tell him than I was a day or even a week ago.

"Penny for your thoughts?"

I jump at Ethan's voice from beside me in bed, and he chuckles as he pulls me on top of his chest.

"You wanna tell me what's running through that pretty head of yours?" he asks again, reaching up to tuck a piece of hair behind my ear.

My body shudders at the slight touch, but it

doesn't distract me from my thoughts like it should. I need to be ready to leave for the airport in an hour, and I still haven't the slightest clue how to tell him I'm leaving.

"Ethan, I..." My voice tapers off as tears well up in my eyes, and I hang my head so he doesn't see my despair.

"This is because you're leaving, right?" His voice is soft as he hooks his thumb under my jaw, gently guiding my eyes back up to meet his.

"How did you—"

"I've known since the day you got here," he explains, a sad little smirk tugging at his mouth. "You do know I have access to the guest book, right?"

"Oh. Right," I murmur, trying to break away from his hold.

"Stop that," he orders, though it sounds more like a plea. "I need you to look at me."

I do as he says, watching his dark eyes scour my face, trying to memorize each dip and curve for when we part. As my first tear threatens to break free, he swoops his thumb over my cheek, catching the drop before it has a chance to fall.

"Don't cry, Freckles. Not for me," he whispers, reaching up to touch his lips to mine. "I can't bear to see you cry."

“I can’t help it,” I admit, leaning down and wrapping my arms around his neck. “I wish I didn’t have to go.”

“Me too, Freckles. Me too,” he groans, flipping me over to my back and crashing his lips to mine. I moan against his mouth, wrapping my legs around his waist and deepening the kiss.

“Fuck me, Ethan. Please,” I gasp, feeling his cock twitch between my thighs.

He chuckles lowly, leaning down to my neck and nipping the delicate skin below my ear.

“Trust me, I’m going to,” he promises with a growl. “I’m going to make sure you never forget the feel of my cock between your legs for as long as you live.”

I cry out as he slams into me, making the rest of the world fade away to bliss.

I hobble down the grand staircase for the last time with my luggage in hand. A numbness had taken over my body when Ethan and I kissed goodbye at the door, and I’m just now starting to come to terms with the reality of the situation.

The bright-pink walls of the lobby seem muted

compared to when I first saw the grand space, and my steps sound muffled to my ears as I stalk across the freshly waxed floors. I step slowly up to the reception desk with a heavy heart, unable to muster up even a small smile as Anna greets me.

"Ready to check out, dear?"

I nod, placing the golden key on the counter and sliding it toward her. She gives me a sad little smile as she pockets it, her eyes squinted with a knowing look.

"You know, if you wanted to stay a little longer, we could—"

"Thank you, Anna," I interrupt, feeling my heart clench as she nods with comprehension. "Could you call a car for me?"

"Of course. It'll be a few minutes if you want to wait in the lobby?"

I shake my head sadly. "Thank you for everything, Anna. You've been more kind to me than you should have...But I think I'm going to wait outside if that's okay."

She nods, her kind eyes full of sympathy. "You take care of yourself, sweetheart."

"I will." I smile, turning toward the exit and making my way outside.

I stand on the pavement, frozen in place as I stare up at the gulls flying overhead, wishing I had an ounce of their freedom.

Must be nice, I think bitterly, casting my eyes away from the sky and focusing on waiting impatiently for the driver. A few endless minutes later, a silver SUV pulls up next to me, and I breathe a sigh of relief as I start to load my bags in the trunk.

"You're heading to the airport, right?" he asks.

Slamming my door closed, I pull the seat belt over my lap and give him a nod in the rearview mirror, still not trusting my voice. Satisfied with the confirmation, he gives me a thumbs-up, then shifts the gear into drive and peels off down the road.

With the bleak reminder of where I'm headed, I start rummaging through my bag in search of my wallet. I haven't even bothered to check if my ID and plane ticket are still tucked safely inside, which is a little alarming, considering I usually triple-check these things.

I breathe a sigh of relief as my hand curls around the small leather wallet, and I immediately rip it open. I use so much force that several of its contents fly onto the floor, and I curse under my breath as I scramble to retrieve them. My fingertips brush against a folded weathered note, and my body freezes as I palm the piece of paper.

Unfolding the delicate note, I bring it up to my face and let my eyes tear over the letters I know by heart, feeling them well with tears as I read.

My sweetest Amelia,

By the time you read this, I will already have gone. This sickness has taken its toll on me, and I want you to know I am at peace, that I accepted my fate long ago, and I've come to terms with what it means.

The truth of the matter is that I've lived a wonderful life; I've loved and been loved, traveled the world and seen every beautiful thing there is to lay eyes on. Most importantly, I've been a mother to the most wonderful daughter a person could ask for, and I will always be grateful for that.

I imagine you're angry, hurt, even devastated, and I want you to know it's okay. Let yourself feel it all, cry for me if you must. But after that, Amelia, I need you to move on.

I know you won't want to—you'll spend months agonizing over everything you could have done to change the situation. But as your mother, who loves you more than you could ever realize, I'm asking you to let me go.

You've lived your life for me, taken care of me in the moments when you most needed someone to take care of you. My illness robbed you of your childhood—even though you would never admit it or blame me for it—but I won't let it steal the life you were meant to lead.

Attached to this letter is a key to a safety deposit box—you'll find everything you need in there to start fresh. Spend it on whatever you want, just make sure it's not all in one place. Find love. Real, true love; because, at the end of the day, it's all that matters in this world.

I love you, my dear, sweet girl. Death could never change that.

I'll give your love to your father.

-W

"Stop the car!" The scream tears through my throat, startling the living piss out of my driver.

"Ma'am, I can't just stop in the middle of the road."

"Then pull over!" I demand, yanking on the handle until the door cracks open.

"Shit, okay! Just wait a second!" he screeches, his eyes wide in horror at the passenger trying to jump out of his moving vehicle.

As soon as the wheels screech to a halt on the shoulder, I yank open the door and sprint back toward the hotel. The driver calls after me, but his cries are a dull buzzing to my ears as my feet fly across the pavement.

I throw open the doors of the Grand Flamingo, drenched in sweat and heaving as Anna looks on in utter confusion.

"My goodness, what happen—"

"I'm sorry, Anna. Do you know where Ethan is?" I ask, trying not to feel bad for cutting her off.

At the mention of his name, her eyes soften.

"The last I saw, he was heading up to your old room. Said he needed to fix something." She gives me a knowing look.

I beam her a little smile of thanks, then turn on my heels toward the stairwell.

"Oh, Ms. Hayes?"

I jump at the soft noise, stopping to face her once more.

"Yes?" I ask.

"Should I assume you'll want to extend your stay?"

My face heats at the twinkle in her eye, and I give her a small nod before running up the stairs. My feet tear in the direction I've come to know this past week, and I only stop when the numbers 201 stare me directly in the face. I pause with my fist wrapped around the handle, debating whether this is a good idea.

Shaking my head, I throw open the door and step inside. Ethan stands with his back to me at the foot of the bed, his shoulders hunched over in a defeated stance I have never seen before.

"Sorry, Anna, I'm coming back down in a seco—" His voice cuts off as he turns to face me, his eyes going wide as he takes in my disheveled appearance.

"Freckles," he breathes, his face lit up with disbelief.

"Hey," I whisper, stepping forward into his chest. "I missed you."

He laughs, wrapping his arms around my shoulders and pulling me tight against his chest.

"But it's only been a few hours," he murmurs, shooting my earlier comment right back at me.

I swat him lightly on the shoulder, nuzzling my head into the crook of his arm and breathing him in.

He delicately rubs his hands across my skin, memorizing each inch of my body with his touch.

"I thought I would never see you again," he whispers, his voice cracking with raw emotion.

"I'm not going anywhere," I whisper. "Not anymore."

"And what brought this change?" he asks, reaching his hand up to cup my cheek.

"Nothing, I—" I stop, anxious whether or not the words I want to say will even come out.

Taking a deep breath, I steel myself against the fireworks exploding in my belly and force myself to look dead into his piercingly dark eyes.

"Ethan, I... I love you."

He pauses, unblinking as he stares straight back at me. Before long, his signature smirk makes its way across his face.

"Are you *nervous,* Freckles?"

Before I have the chance to respond, he pulls me in close, his hand cupping the back of my neck as he leans down to whisper in my ear.

"Well, I find that ridiculous. Because, you see...I've been trying to find the courage to tell you the same thing."

"You mean..."

"I *mean,*" he echoes, pulling my chin up to meet

his gaze, "that I love you, Amelia. I have since that first day I looked into those big brown eyes of yours. Amelia Hayes, if you'll have me—"

Ethan's eyes go wide as I spring up, kissing him hard and effectively cutting him off.

"Before you keep going," I start, pulling back and giving Ethan a cheesy grin, "I love you too, Ethan Stone. But then, you already knew that."

Before I can say another word, Ethan pulls me into a deep kiss, his arms wrapped around my waist and pulling my body closer to him.

"You talk too much, you know that?" He grins down at me, his dark eyes filled with deep, swirling emotion.

"Yeah, I think I've heard that once or twice." I giggle, a small blush forming over the apples of my cheeks.

"Although..." he muses, forcing my chin up to him with his index finger. "I can't seem to get enough of it, now, can I?"

"Well, I'm glad." I laugh again, looking up at him with a mischievous glint.

"Although..." I trail off.

"What?"

"I think this whole thing would be better if... you know."

"Know what?"

"If you kiss me again."

After letting out another booming chuckle, his eyes bright and filled with happiness, he does.

Over and over and over again.

Epilogue

2 YEARS LATER

As soon as we break away from each other, Ethan pulls me into another deep kiss, knowing full well we're supposed to exchange just *one* after the vows.

"Whoop, whoop!" Liz cheers, effectively breaking us out of our spell.

I shoot her a glare with flaming cheeks, but she just rolls her eyes while crossing her arms over her satin bridesmaid dress.

"Dude, you guys can make out all you want later, but some of us are ready to start drinking!" Liz chuckles, shooting Ethan and me a wink.

"Everyone's free to go!" Ethan calls out, then leans down to kiss the crook of my neck.

"I need some more time with my wife," he hums lowly against my ear.

I lean into him, feeling a familiar warmth spread across my chest as he places delicate kisses along my collarbone. He pulls back, and I look up, resting my chin on his chest with a concerned glance at the tears welling up in his eyes.

"What are those for?" I whisper.

"For you, Mrs. Stone." He chuckles, kissing my cheek as he blinks the tears away. "You have made me the happiest man today," he chokes out, his pupils blowing as he stares down at me.

"Ditto," I whisper, leaning into his tight embrace as my heart swells.

"As much as I would like nothing more than to whisk you away right now," Ethan groans, "I think we should make an appearance at our wedding reception. Plus, someone has to keep an eye on Liz," he adds, winking down at me playfully.

"What can you do? She's my best friend." I chuckle lightly, placing a delicate kiss against his suit-clad chest.

"Let's go, Mr. Stone." I break away, smiling brightly and gesturing toward the direction of the bar.

"Right after you, Mrs. Stone," Ethan drawls, intertwining his fingers with mine and placing a kiss against my bright-pink cheek.

Do you want to know Ethan's first thoughts as

badly as Amelia did? Join my #Grouples newsletter to read HIS perspective from their meet cute.

Curious about Amelia's best friend, Liz? Her story is next in Broken & Bound!

About the Author

Mindy Paige was born and raised in Florida. She started writing at a young age. After getting her degree in botany, she decided to pursue her dream of being an author. Her debut romance novel, Time and Tide, was written while finishing her senior year of college.

If not writing or reading, Mindy can usually be found playing with her dogs, tending to her plants, watching reality television with her boyfriend, or painting.

Don't miss out on release news and giveaways; join Mindy's newsletter!

Made in the USA
Columbia, SC
03 February 2025

52591710R00117